BEAUTIFUL AND DAMNED

OTHER BOOKS BY ROBERT M. DRAKE

SPACESHIP (2012)

SCIENCE (2013)

BEAUTIFUL CHAOS (2014)

BLACK BUTTERFLY (2015)

A BRILLIANT MADNESS (2015)

BEAUTIFUL & DAMNED

STORIES

ROBERT M. DRAKE

Printed in the
United States Of America
ISBN: 978-0-9862627-7-7

Book Design: Robert M. Drake

First Edition 2016

Contact: RMDRKONE@gmail.com

Special Thanks to Whitney Bryson & Jennifer Bassil.
You both dug me out of the grave.

To Sevyn,

It has been a pleasure meeting
you in this life.

It brings me joy to know that you found me.
When you are a woman
read these words and know that most,
if not all, were inspired by you.

I love you. I love you. I love you.

Thank you for being you.

This book will not contain any images.
This time, you'll have to draw them all in your head.

BEAUTIFUL & DAMNED

STORIES

And then
you became that place
I couldn't visit anymore,
that song
I couldn't listen to,
that memory
I couldn't relive,
that one night
I couldn't go back to.

You became everything
I wish I had.

CONTENTS

We are all running away
or towards something kid,
let us just hope whatever
it is we crash into does not
make the day dimmer
and the night darker.

You deserve at least
ten thousand suns.

We all do.

BEAUTIFUL AND DAMNED

Too many faces,
too many places,
many things within many things
and in so many ways
they could all inspire your life,
if only,
you gave them all
a chance.

BEAUTIFUL & DAMNED

STORIES

ROBERT M. DRAKE

You seemed fine
the last time we spoke.
You seemed better,
as if somewhere in this
endless dark space
you found a map,
and it led you
out of this world.

I hope you find what
you're looking for.

I hope you come back soon.

THE BEAUTIFUL

BE GENTLE. BE KIND.

ALL OF ME

1

In the midst of an emotional breakdown, Angela felt as if her life was nothing more than a collection of meaningless events filled with meaningless people. Six months ago, she moved to New York City for a new job and all the excitement that the city had to offer. But nothing was going as she'd planned. She felt overwhelmed at work. New friendships never panned out. The weather never befriended her, and sometimes she missed home.

It was this day, after one too many emails filled with complaints, one too many phone calls from rude customers, that she finally reached the tipping point.

"That's it. I can't take it anymore!" She slammed down the phone receiver and stormed out of the office.

A few moments later, she was in a bathroom stall sobbing. With the same loyalty as the people she met in the city, many co-workers heard her as they passed the restroom, but none went to her aid. A half hour had

passed, and finally, she took a deep breath, wiped her
tears, and returned to her desk. In that short time,
emails flooded her inbox and countless messages jammed
her phone. Ignoring everything, she just sat there.
Each new email, each ring of the phone, added more
pressure. Although the crying helped, her overwhelming
frustration shot to full tilt and without much thought,
she walked into her boss' office in a silent outrage.

"I quit!" she yelled.

"Angela, what's wrong?" asked her boss. Unlike most
bosses, he cared for the well being of his employees.
Angela was a good worker and he didn't want to lose
her. She was smart, she was reliable, and she rarely
complained, which was why this news shocked him.

"I've had enough. I can't take it anymore." The fury
in her eyes was hard to miss.

"Why don't you take the week off and then we can
talk about this? Okay?" he said, trying to calm her
down.

"No, I'm done. I'm leaving." She thundered out of
his office, grabbed her things, and left, as a trail of
anger and regret followed her out the door. She knew
her co-workers would gossip, but she didn't care. She
didn't like any of them anyway. Work was one huge
competition and they were out to eliminate her, or so

she thought. Either way, she didn't care. She just wanted to get out of there.

With her belongings in tow, she stomped out of the building and hurried to her car. She felt good, somewhat liberated. She couldn't believe that she'd just quit and for once, she felt like she was in control.

Once in her car, Angela took in a few deep breaths and tried to relax. Her hands trembled and her mind spun. And because of that, she decided to take the train home.

2

On the crowded isolation of the train, she considered moving back home. From a small town in North Carolina, her dream was to live in the Big Apple, but reality and fantasy were two different things. New York City was not how she envisioned it would be. Her life was all work. She barely had any time to go anywhere, make real friends, or try anything new. Worst of all, she always had work to finish at home, and there was no end to this cycle.

Jammed into the corner of the train, barely hanging on to the rail, Angela couldn't even escape by looking out the window. Strangers pushed against her. The stench of sweat assaulted her. Finally, the train approached her stop, and she rang the bell. The bus lurched to a stop and Angela picked up her things and got off the bus.

As she walked home, she felt heavy, so heavy that each step was a chore. She realized that she got off the bus an entire block before her actual stop. Considering she lugged a box full of papers, souvenirs, old pictures and more, she had quite a walk. A wave of people filled the sidewalk. Some walked fast, others strolled, while the rest stood there waiting for god knows what.

She thought the day couldn't get any worse until a distracted man, yelling into his phone, bumped into her, knocking the box to the ground.

"I'm so terribly sorry," he said as he kneeled down to help her retrieve her things.

"No, it's okay, it's not your fault. I wasn't looking," she replied, collecting her things from the pavement.

"Well, there you go . . . good as new," he said as the final contents were placed inside the box.

"Thank you. Really." she said.

"I know this is none of my business, but are you okay? You look like you've had a rough day," he said, and she smiled.

It *was* a bad day, a terrible day, perhaps one of the worst days of her life. Her dream was shattered. She had no idea what she'd do next. She was lost between the city and the shadowy place where regrets dwelled.

"Would you like to grab a coffee?" he said.

His smile flattered her. "When, now?" she asked.

"Yes, why not? Let's go, c'mon, it's on me. Then you can tell me why your mascara has smeared."

She didn't realize her makeup had been ruined. She must have looked like a crazy person when she'd grabbed her belongings and fumed out of the office.

"Don't worry, it's just coffee," he said.

His smile was gentle and it offered her hope. He was quite handsome and had a bit of an old charm. It was something she didn't see these days, so she was instantly impressed.

"You know what? I'll take you up on your offer," she said as she took the box and threw it in an almost filled garbage container.

He liked her quirkiness. He thought it was adorable.

"I'm James," he said as he extended his hand.

"I'm Angela," she replied as she shook his hand with ease.

"Well then, Angela, shall we go? The best coffee in town awaits us."

She nodded her head as if it were a game and sweetly giggled. The small spark in her eyes was alluring.

"I'm kidding, you know you can't find a decent cup of coffee anywhere in the city." He smiled again.

Her eyes lit up when he smiled. Something about him intrigued her. She didn't know what it was, but she was interested. She didn't want to make it too obvious—that would be improper, and well, she wasn't the kind of girl that would easily say what she felt. It took a little more than a smile and a bit of wit and charm, but nonetheless, she was entertained. And she loved it.

"Well then, the worst cup of coffee awaits, let's find it," she said as her energy evenly matched his and they both went off into the borough looking for the worst cup of coffee the city had to offer.

3

Branded with old rustic scraps of metal plastered on the walls, the coffee house had long spiral fans and lights the size of softballs hanging from the edge of each ceiling beam. She thought it was fun and silly to be doing such a thing, but deep down inside, she was still enraged about what had happened earlier that day. Not just anything or anyone would have been able to dazzle her, but he had an alluring sparkle in his eyes and she was captivated. She couldn't remember when the last time was that she felt this way. She felt inspired as he grasped her attention--as if he had been waiting for her his entire life.

They both ordered and decided to sit outside on the edge of the shop where it was quiet.

"So tell me, what's on your mind?" He asked with a sincerity that bloomed in his eyes.

"I just quit my job." She grabbed her cup of coffee, placed it in front of her on the table, and began to stir it. Two cubes of sugar dissolved from the top to the bottom.

"You just quit your job?"

"Yes, about 40 minutes ago. I was in a fury, a wild one. I felt as if I was in control, but then, felt as if I wasn't. I have let too much slip through the cracks. I couldn't take it anymore. Maybe I snapped and tomorrow I'll regret it. But I had no choice. It was bound to happen either way. I felt it in my bones," she said as she twirled the straw in her coffee.

For a moment, he thought about how he would reply. He didn't know what to say or think, he hadn't been put in such a predicament for so long, but still, something inside of him felt as if he had to be comforting no matter what.

"Maybe this is just a cycle for you," he said.

"What do you mean by that? A cycle?"

"Yeah, I mean, you're on the edge, and you took a leap of faith. It's kind of what just happened to me earlier today and maybe that's why we crossed paths. Maybe we both jumped at the same time but in different places," he offered.

"What happened?" she said as her eyes locked with his. She rapidly tapped her foot as if she was nervous, but she wasn't. In fact, she felt an urge to know what it was he had gone through, what it was that led him to her or vice versa. And at that moment, as he opened his mouth to explain what it was that led him to her, she was consumed. She was drawn to him--the same way lovers rush into one another. The same way hands find other

hands in the middle of the night. And with all her
attention, she listened.

"Yeah, I mean, I was supposed to attend a meeting
with a client of mine, but something didn't feel right.
I pretty much backed out of it at the last minute. I
was getting off the elevator--I don't know what it was,
but something felt off and I always trust my gut."

"So what did you do?" Intrigued by his story, she
tried to analyze almost every aspect of James. The
masculine scent of his cologne, the choppy cut of his
dark hair, and the way his lips moved when he spoke. "I
turned around and left, and then, well, I bumped into
you and your box hit me in the gut," he said and he
laughed and then her laughter followed his.

She enjoyed his company, and as he spoke,
she blocked the world out. She was struck by the
sensuous sound of his voice--it was soft like warm
spring rain. She noticed how her day was beginning to
feel a little less frigid. She wanted more of him and
more of his warmth.

They were in the coffee shop for almost 2 hours. The
day was bright; she felt bright, and the spark in his
eyes was far brighter than anything she had ever seen.
She was beginning to feel a kind-heartedness she hadn't
felt in a long time. Radiating from her heart, his
sweetness comforted her and gave her hope. With every
breath, she felt as if she was walking blindly and the

only thing guiding her was his voice. And as she walked deeper into the day, into his light, she was acutely aware how off-balanced she felt. She understood how simple it was to fall, but she also knew how simple it was to rise. And as she sat there listening to James share his story, her heart began to blossom and began to fall.

4

James amused Angela. Everything about him pulled her into him. The way he presented himself, the way he thought, spoke, and the way he made her feel. It was as if the world had been hiding him from her and he had broken free to find her.

As they sat there, he was highly attentive to her. He listened and took all of her feelings under consideration. He made her laugh, and, for a time, she forgot about the terrible experiences she had endured while living in New York City. He took her fragility to a place where it was okay for her to be herself. Where it was okay to wake up and feel miserable and not have it all together. A place where she could accept all her faults, because after all, he thought that was what made her interesting.

"Well then, I guess I should get going," James said as he grabbed a napkin, picked their empty cups up, and wiped the table.

"Already?" Angela gasped. Her eyes grew bigger and her brows raised a notch. She didn't want her time with James to end. He brought out her confidence, her ability to connect, and he made her want to slowly tiptoe across the summer sky and dance.

"Yes, I have to get going, Angela. It was truly an honor and a pleasure," he said as he waited for her to get up from her chair. She tried to come up with an excuse to keep him around, even if it was only for a little while longer.

"Would you like to hang out a while? I don't live far," she said.

He felt a little uncomfortable though he didn't make it obvious.

"I would like to, but I have to go." He opened the door, and they were back on the street." I can take you home. I want to make sure everything is okay with you," he said.

"You don't have to," she said, her tone was light-hearted and carefree. She *did* want him to take her home; she *did* want someone to make sure everything was okay with her. And above all, she *did* want someone to look out for her the same way she looked out for herself.

"Yes, yes I do," he replied.

BEAUTIFUL AND DAMNED

It was that moment when she began to believe in fate and how everything was meant to be. It almost made sense for her. She thought about her move to New York and how she hadn't met anyone or felt any connection to someone since she had gotten there. It had all led to her quitting her job, then, into the presence of something rare. And at that moment, the moment he said, *yes, yes I do*, she finally recognized the soul within his eyes and in an instant; she had fallen, fallen completely, with no way to escape, and no one to ask for help. She, out of all the people in the city, had finally felt a spark, one that was essential for the flame of true love.

"Okay," she said demurely.

"Okay then, shall we go?" he said and as they both they headed toward James' car.

The entire drive home Angela was quiet and it wasn't because she didn't have anything to say, but rather, she had so much to say that she didn't know where to begin. She was filled with melody and it silently flew out of her like a bird shooting up toward the sky. She wanted to laugh and play. She felt like a small child rolling around in the grass.

"You're awfully quiet," he said as he turned his light signal and made a left.

"Yes, I'm fine, just thinking." Her head leaned toward the passenger window as she looked outside.

"What's on your mind?"

"Nothing really, I'm just thinking. Hey, make a right at the stop sign and then keep going straight," she said. There wasn't any traffic, which they both found to be odd.

"Okay." He didn't think much of her silence. He just kept on driving as he hummed a sweet little jazz number.

"What song is that?" she asked.

He placed both of his hands on the wheel. He took a deep breath as if the song was a complete secret and perhaps it was.

"It's "All of Me," by Billie Holiday. Do you know anything about her?"

"I'm afraid I don't. I'll look her up as soon as I get home."

"You've *never* heard of Billie Holiday?" His smile broadened. "I highly recommend her; she's sort of the bee's knees of Jazz." He looked out his rear view mirror and accelerated a little.

"Make one more left. I live in the red apartments, the ones with the wooden gate and security standing in front of them." Her heart fluttered. "And okay, I'll remember her name and I'll get back to you on that."

The car came to a complete stop right in front of the wooden gate. And then she remembered something that was crucial to her.

"Shoot, I left my car at work! Shoot!" Her hands clapped, and her left foot pressed against the base of James car.

"Do you want me to take you so you can get it?"

"No, it's okay, it's my fault. I'll hitch a ride from my neighbor in the morning. It's okay. I promise." She smiled as she spoke and James smiled back.

"Are you sure? I mean, it's not a big deal," he offered.

"I'm sure." She stared into James' eyes. She wasn't too worried about her car. She knew that was a minor problem. What she *was* thinking about was James--whether or not he would ask her for her number, or at least a proper night out.

He sensed she had something on her mind and wasn't blind to the fact of what it was she wanted. And there was no doubt that perhaps, he wanted the same thing.

They sat there in silence for a few seconds. The silence was the excruciatingly loud.

"Well, this is my stop. I guess this is our goodbye? Right?" She wanted more of James. She wanted to see him again, to learn more about his past, to understand what inspired him and what hurt him. She wanted to be more than just that girl he once took for coffee. She wanted to be more than just a memory.

"Yes, this is it, Angela." His words carefully exited his lips and his eyes tensed a little as if he had something else to say. And then, Angela just did it. She asked him; she asked him that one question that had been lingering in her mind, in her heart. She wasn't the type of girl to do such a thing, but he had come into her life during a breaking point, and because of that, anything was possible, even her doing such things she wouldn't have normally done. Besides that, she felt a connection with James and perhaps it was the one she had been long yearning for, ever since she had arrived in New York.

"Will I ever see you again?" she said as her right hand touched her face and her teeth gently pressed upon her bottom lip. She slowly smiled. She was embarrassed and shy to ask, but she had no other option. Something inside of her had pushed her off the edge.

BEAUTIFUL AND DAMNED

James glanced away. He took a gulp and flinched a little. "No Angela, as much as I want to, I can't. It wouldn't be right."

She was at a loss for words, and once again the gloom slammed around her. She had been let down one too many times. She thought that she would see James again. Her face turned red and what remained of her mascara began to run again. She had already been devastated earlier today and because of that, she was very emotional.

"Oh God, this was clearly a mistake. I'm so sorry for asking." She quickly turned away and fumbled to open the car door.

"No, wait." He grabbed her hand. She sat there but didn't look at him. She just listened to what he had to say hoping that maybe it wasn't as bad as she thought it might be.

"The thing is, I'm seeing someone and it's not right to agree to see you again. We both know that's not the way things should be."

As his words flowed like a choppy ocean, they began to set her off again, and it was the same way she had blown a fuse earlier. She, once again, found herself at a boiling point.

"Then why all of this James? We just had a wonderful time and for what? To end it like this? I enjoyed our company together and I don't believe in coincidence. I was supposed to meet you don't you get it? And now you tell me this? Gosh! My day keeps getting worse and worse. I mean, why did you spend the time with me? Why?"

She didn't want to overexaggerate, but it was true. "Why had James invited her to coffee? Was this some kind of sick game?" Angela thought.

James knew he wasn't the type of guy to meddle around with someone else's feelings, for he too had felt something for Angela, and it was the same feeling two people feel when they are confronted with something greater than themselves.

"I did it because you needed someone to be there for you, even if it was for a little while. I saw you the moment you jumped on the train and when I saw you, it was as if a miracle had happened. And I know it sounds ridiculous, but it's true. I wanted to meet you and talk to you and live in your world for a while, and to be honest, to me, that's better than you just being another girl on the train. I can now go on--knowing someone like you exists in the world, even if I never see you again, my life will be better because of you. Because I know you'll be out there. And you know, I'm okay with that, that's good enough for me. And that's why I did it and I'm sorry to have let you down. But I can't. Not like this. I'm sorry Angela; it's not the right time."

She didn't say a word as she climbed out of his car. She ran straight into her apartment, confused. She didn't know what was going on today and for a moment, she thought she had gone a little mad. It was too much for her to deal with. It was all too much for one day. Devastated because of her job and her connection with James, she closed her windows, turned on a CD and escaped the world.

5

As time passed, she eventually forgot about her last job and got a new one. She went on, with James being a distant memory. She met other people throughout the rest of the year. It had been a little over a year since she had met James and although she was over the incident, occasionally something would happen and she'd be reminded of him. The smell of coffee brewing in the afternoon, the sound of the train as it came and went, and sometimes she would play Billie Holiday singing "All of Me." His face would appear every time she thought of him and she wondered what had become of him and that's where it would end.

"I have to go to the store, and yes, I'll be there next week," Angela said as she laughed over the phone. She was talking to her mother who was back home in

North Carolina. It was about a week before Thanksgiving
and Angela planned to fly back to see her.

"Okay, Mom. I'll talk to you later. I have to go.
It's snowing here and I don't want to get caught in a
storm. Love you, Mom. Tell dad I said hi. I can't wait
to see you guys." She hung up the phone, grabbed her
keys, and went to the store.

The city was already filled with Christmas lights
and the holiday spirit was at full steam. It was
everywhere, especially within Angela. She was cheerful
and ecstatic about going back home for the holiday.

She entered C-towns Supermarket and, as usual, it
pulled a crowd. She had to wait in line to get in, and
by the time she did, she was so cold she had to stand
beneath their heaters to warm up. She grabbed a cart
and then got the bare minimum to last until she headed
to North Carolina.

After fighting the crowd in the store, Angela
stepped into the cashier line to pay for her items.

"Angela?"

The voice wasn't familiar at all. She turned around,
clearing her bangs from her eyes and a tall man with a
beard stood behind her. He wore a white long sleeve
shirt with a teal-colored tie.

BEAUTIFUL AND DAMNED

"Angela? Don't you recognize me?" he said, juggling a bag full of groceries.

And then, it just came to her: last year, the coffee shop, and Billie Holiday-the memories avalanched.

"James?"

"That smile hasn't changed. You haven't changed. How have you been?"

They stood in the middle of the line: one person ahead of her, three behind him. Shocked, Angela didn't know what to say.

"You look lovely," James said.

"I've been good. My god, it's been so long. You look great too."

"So, you're getting ready for Thanksgiving?" he blurted, not really knowing what to say.

She waved her bangs towards the back of her ears again and looked behind her shoulder as if she was nervous, but again, she wasn't nervous, not at all.

"Yes, I'm going to visit my family in North Carolina. I'm leaving in a few days, how about you?"

"I'm flying out. San Francisco. I'm going to visit my sister. She just moved to Sausalito."

"That sounds like fun. I hope you enjoy yourself." She took a few steps closer to the cashier.

"Yeah . . . I hope so, too."

"Well, it was nice seeing you James. I hope you have a wonderful holiday." She felt a sting coming from the bottom of her heart. It reminded her of that day, the day she had met him and thought he was the one who was bound to save her from what was then a desperate life.

"Yeah, you too, Angela." Something inside of him felt broken. Although the holiday spirit fluttered throughout the city, it wasn't touching him. Something in James was missing. He smiled at Angela one last time and headed back to the line he was originally in. And then, as he took several steps, a song began to play, his favorite. It was "All of Me" by Billie Holiday. The song drifted throughout the store's speakers. This was indeed an act of fate, James thought. Seeing Angela was not a coincidence. Everything happens for a reason, he thought as he reflected on the fact that almost every night since he'd met Angela, he terribly regretted cutting her off the way he had. He quickly turned around and headed straight toward Angela.

BEAUTIFUL AND DAMNED

"Angela . . ." he said as Billie Holiday played in the backdrop. He walked toward her and gently tapped her on the shoulder.

Angela turned around and smiled. She was thinking how the two of them, being there while this song was playing, was no coincidence.

And then, without Angela having to ask, James did what she had been waiting for him to do since the first day they met.

"I want to see you again. Can I see you again?"

Overwhelmed by what she had just heard. She said the first thing that came to her mind. "Billie Holiday!" she murmured as the cashier began to check out her items.

"Yes, Billie Holiday. You recognize her now?" he said with fire in his eyes.

"Yes, yes I do. She's kind of the bee's knees of Jazz, and this song so happens to be my favorite." She began to hum the melody the same way James had hummed the song over a year ago. She hadn't forgotten when he first spoke to her. And he, too, hadn't forgotten the moment she came onto the train.

"This song is my favorite, too," he said, unable to disguise the desire he now felt. "Can I see you again? Perhaps, when you get back from your trip?"

"I don't know; I have to think about it." She smiled and then she turned away and then turned back and smiled at James again. But it wasn't a full smile, but it was a good smile. Of course she wanted to see him again. After all, she hadn't truly forgotten him either.

"So is that a yes?" he asked.

"Yes, yes I'll see you again. Now let me pay for my groceries and we'll talk about this later." Her cheeks flushed red and the warmth within her surfaced, like a single flower bursting into bloom, in a quiet field.

"So may I have your number, Angela?"

"No, you may not."

"No?"

"Because fate has a funny way of mending things back together. I mean, you are here, and I am here, and we'll find each other again, that is, if that's the way it's supposed to be. So if you believe, and I believe, too--some way, somehow, we'll find each other again. Okay? Well, I have to go now. Goodbye, James." She paid the cashier and waited for her change.

James felt abandoned. He didn't know how to react. His mouth was agape as he slowly faded out of his body. He couldn't move; he just stood there with a bag full of groceries in his hands as he watched Angela leave out of his life for the second time.

6

James arrived home, crushed at what had just happened. For the past year, he had continuously thought about how he would greet Angela if ever he ran into her again. He didn't expect her just to leave and especially in such a way that left him out in the cold. A profound sadness poured over him. He tried to let it go and immersed himself in organizing his groceries in the fridge.

Later that evening, he emptied his pockets and a slip of paper with a phone number came out with his change. No name. Curious and hopeful, he grabbed his cell phone and dialed in.

It rang four times before someone picked up the phone.

"Hello," said a woman on the other end.

"Hello . . ." said James.

"How could I help you?" said the woman.

"My name is James and I found this number and I was just curious as to who it was. I'm sorry if I bothered you madam."

The woman didn't speak and in the middle of nowhere an acquainted voice sputtered through the phone.

"James, you found me. I told you we'd find each other."

"I knew this number led to you. I felt it and I trusted my gut with it and that's why I called it."

"How did you know?"

"Because ever since I saw you, I knew, and I knew I would find you. To tell you..."

"To tell me what?" Angela cut him off before he could finish his sentence.

"To tell you, that day, in the coffee shop, that day, I fell into you and I'm sorry I'm late, but hey, coincidences don't exist, right?"

"No, I'm afraid they don't."

"Then I'll see you later, will I? James said.

"Only if fate allows it," said Angela.

"Oh, I think it will, Angela."

"I think so too. So where do we go from here?"
Angela said as she walked around her apartment in
twirl.

"Anywhere, as long as you're with me, from here on
out."

ALONG CAME A SPIDER

1

I didn't drive. Not because I didn't have a car or a license but because I didn't like the idea of being inside a box with four wheels, surrounded by other people trapped in other boxes with other four wheels. Because of this, I took the train, the bus, or rode my bicycle whenever I needed to. Walking was a last resort. It was worse than driving. One of my best friends got himself killed walking. He was on the sidewalk when a car accidentally hit him. I guess, this was why I didn't like cars or walking.

I was already late. My friend had invited me to have lunch with him and a handful of our friends. I walked down 8th and Flagler Street to the bus stop, right in front of the university. I had been waiting at the bus stop for nearly 15 minutes. Of course, it felt longer. When you had to wait for over 10 minutes for anything, the minutes would drag.

I was supposed to be there at noon. Being late makes me panicky, and having to wait, while being late, was worse. It wasn't in my character to be late and yet, I had forgotten about this get-together and only remembered it about 30 minutes ago.

To my surprise, there was no one sitting here with me and I found that to be odd. Every time I passed this stop, it was always filled with people. I wondered why it was so empty today, on a Tuesday, about a quarter past noon. There was no sunshine. No city noise. No cars passing by. It didn't feel like an ordinary day. Something was different and forgetting a lunch date was the first sign. Strange things could happen when you are alone and by that, I mean anything could happen when you're alone. But it's not like I was expecting a tornado to drift me into Oz. No, not that, although that would be a marvelous story to tell.

Time passed and finally, a student arrived. I could tell he was a student by his book-bag and he limped as he pulled a suitcase. Maybe it wasn't a suitcase; I'm not sure. It looked as if he had a musical instrument in there. When he got to the bus stop, he just dropped everything as if it were dead weight, something of no use to him. He sighed. He was a pretty big guy, by that I mean heavy. He was maybe about 6" 1', 300, maybe even 400 pounds. He wore old headphones and obnoxiously loud techno music blasted from them. God, it was awful. I don't understand how anyone could develop such a taste for that kind of music. He looked at me and didn't say a word. I glanced back and quickly turned away, minding

my own business. The last thing I needed was small
talk. I hated small talk; it cheapened everything.

"You got a light?" the kid asked as this awful scent
of old earth and dry skin radiated from his clothes. He
smelled terrible; I wasn't sure how I didn't catch that
sooner.

"Uh no, I don't smoke, sorry," I replied as I tucked
both of my feet beneath the bench.

"Well, that's good. Smoking can kill you," he said.

What terrible humor, I thought. *A smoker telling a
non-smoker not to smoke because smoking could
potentially kill you?* How do you detach yourself from
that? This guy made no sense whatsoever, but that in
itself interested me. I took a leap and began to talk
to him and it was something I normally didn't do.

"So, what are you listening to?"

"Prodigy," he said as his head rocked back and
forth. I thought it was rather strange the way his head
bobbed like it was attached to a spring.

"Wow, I haven't heard Prodigy in forever."

"Yeah, they're awesome," he said as he continued to
bebop. I didn't know what to think of this guy.

Suddenly, he grabbed his book bag and searched through it.

"I got one!" he shouted in victory as if he had just won a contest.

"Got what?"

"Some matches," he said as he took an old box of matches out and lit the cigarette up.

"This makes waiting for the bus so much easier." He took a few tokes and blew the smoke in the other direction. Even so, the wind slowly swept it toward my face and I held my breath until it passed.

A girl walked toward the bus stop carrying a briefcase. She was about 5'2", maybe around 100 pounds, and had enchanting brown hair with auburn streaks. The way she walked made it difficult not to notice her sinewy legs. Once she was close enough, I could see her gray eyes that looked like the moon when it was full.

"Hey," said the kid with the techno music as she sat on the edge of the bench, to my left.

"Hi," she said with a shy smile. She placed the briefcase on the ground and shoved a handful of papers into the side pocket.

"Hi, I'm Adrian." I extended my hand to greet her. This was something I normally didn't do, but like I said, I was panicky, and being so can make you do things, unexpected things.

"Hi Adrian, I'm Rayne," she said, her voice like rose petals, soft and bouncy.

I thought that was an unusual name. I mean, really, what kind of parent would name their child Rain? I had never heard of such a name. I mean, it didn't sound awful, no, not at all, but it was rather left-sided. She must have had it bad in grade school. I could instantly think of a million different ways to make fun of her name.

The techno kid pulled a little brown box from his suitcase. He opened it to reveal a pile of little white squares of candy.

"Does anyone want some bubble gum?" He extended his arm toward Rayne and me. We looked at each other for a moment--I think because it was so random, the way the techno kid asked. You know, we've all heard about taking candy from strangers, besides that, it was such an awkward thing to ask.

"It's special gum; it's not from around here," he insisted. I thought about it but not much. It was a piece of gum: nothing more, nothing less.

"Okay, I'll have one." I reached into the small wooden box for a piece. Rayne did the same.

We continued to talk about school, politics, sports, music and several other things. It made the wait bearable. Plus, the more time I spent with these strangers, the more I felt like being late to my friend's lunch wasn't such a bad thing after all.

2

I glanced at my watch. My god, I *was* late. Where the hell was that bus? I was definitely going to hear it from my friends. A late bus wasn't really an excuse. I could have hopped on my bike a half hour ago, but the conversation was so--well, I wasn't about to go back home, after all, I'd been waiting at the bus stop for over an hour.

"Help me!"

The voice seemed to come from the dumpster near the lake in front of the university.

"Did you guys hear that?" I asked Rayne.

Engrossed in a book, she shook her head and the techno guy still jammed to his music. He didn't even hear me ask the question.

"Help me, someone please help me!" The voice was even louder, and it was indeed coming from the direction of the garbage. I got up to check it out.

"Where are you going?" Rayne asked as she put her book down and placed it over her legs.

"You didn't hear that? Someone yelled for help. It was loud and clear." I said as I took a few steps towards the garbage.

"You're crazy. I didn't hear anything." She said as she shook her head again, but this time, it was a faint shake as if I *were* crazy.

"Well, I'm going to check it out. I'll be back."

"Okay, we'll be here. Don't wander away too far. You don't want to miss the bus. You'll be even later to your friend's lunch. After all, you've been panicking about it the past hour or so." She lifted her book and went back to reading it as I continued to walk towards the garbage.

"Help me; it's going to kill me. Someone help me!" The distressed voice was almost a scream. The closer I got to the garbage, the more I began to think who it could be. Perhaps a homeless fighting another, this wasn't something new to the eyes around this side of town. Sometimes the unfortunate would stand by the university to ask for donations and it wasn't unusual

to see one or two of them fight over a particularly
lucrative spot.

"Help me! Someone get me out of here."

I walked faster and then broke into a jog. I almost
lost my balance. The voice was right around the corner.
I didn't know why I was doing this and I had no idea
what I'd do if someone were being attacked, but
something inside of me seemed to push me, and I wasn't
sure what it was. I just got up--and I'm no hero--but
if there were someone to save or anything out of my
comfort zone to do, then, perhaps, a different side of
me would emerge and explode like a hot grenade in mid
air.

"Help . . ." the voice sounded as if it were gasping
for air. I circled the garbage twice and saw no one.
And then, as I stomped my feet, a black cat rushed out
from beneath the garbage with a little red fish in its
mouth. It spooked me and then I kind of spooked the
cat. It dropped the fish on the ground and vanished
into the university campus.

"Thanks for the help, kid." I looked around to see
who was talking. Nothing. I peeked around the edge of
the dumpster and still, I saw nothing.

"Hey kid, down here."

I looked down and took a few steps back.

"Over here, can't you hear me? Get me in water. I can't breathe."

I looked down. It was the little red fish flapping on the ground.

"A little help here, kid? Grab that half-gallon milk carton popping out from the recycle container and run towards the lake, fill it up with water and come back-- put me in it. Think you could do that for me, kid? I'm barely hanging on here."

I snapped out of my trance. "Right!" I opened the recycle container, grabbed the half-gallon milk carton and ran towards the lake. I filled it with water and rushed back to save the little fish. I gently grabbed it and slid it into the milk carton filled with lake water.

"Why didn't you just ask me to place you back in the lake? And how come you're talking?" Of course, those were the two obvious things to ask. One, why would a fish want to be placed in a carton or a tank or anything else that would prevent it from being wild? And two, why was it talking?

"Well, to answer both of your questions-one, I don't want to go back to the lake, that's how I ended up in this mess, and two--English is the international language of the world," said the fish as it replenished itself in the water.

35

"That's just ridiculous, isn't it? That is, English being the international language of the world. Why not speak another language or why use language at all." I asked, thinking what I must look like having a conversation with a fish in a milk carton. "Why not some other kind of communication? Perhaps, thought-to-thought transfer? After all, you're not moving your little fish mouth the same way I am moving mine to express these words." I said as I lifted the milk carton closer to my face. I looked toward the bus stop and saw Rayne and the techno kid still preoccupied.

"So kid, listen, because you saved me. I am going to grant you a wish."

"A wish?"

"Yes, you heard me, a wish, but just one, and you cannot wish for more wishes. That's against the rules," said the fish.

"The rules? *What* are you?" I asked as I shook the milk carton a little.

"Hey, kid, don't do that. It makes me dizzy."

I tried to stabilize the carton.

"What am I?" the fish repeated. "Well, how can I explain it? I'm a djinn and I've been cursed. Punished. Turned me into a damn fish. Although, the last time I was a rat and got killed by a hideous cat. And before that, I was a tiger and was shot dead by a poacher and before that, I was a gorilla--a poacher got me, again. I can't remember what I was before that, sorry. Either way, if someone saves me, then I grant them a wish and as you can see I haven't been granting any wishes within the last few decades. So, at last, you are my first fish-wish in this century, so make it a good one."

"Well, I don't believe you. It sounds impossible, and you talking to me *is* impossible. This isn't even happening." I said that because I had been waiting for the bus for so long-and the anxiety had been pounding at me. Was I beginning to be delusional? "I'm just going to place you back where I found you. Actually, I'm going to place you in the lake and let's just call that even? Deal?"

"Listen, kid. I'm afraid it's not that simple. You either make the wish or terrible things will happen. Things you won't be able to understand and they won't stop, not until your wish is granted." Said the red fish as its voice darkened and its eyes glowed red like the blood it had spilled in its previous lives.

I didn't believe a word the fish said. I walked toward the lake and placed it back in the water. I didn't care what it said. To me, it meant nothing. Although, a fish speaking fluent English was as bizarre as it got, but like I said, I was late, and although the conversation with Rayne and the techno kid had been nice, the panic was clawing at me. I didn't care what the delusion was saying; there was nothing to stop me from putting the fish back where it belonged.

As I walked back to the bus stop, I glanced back to the lake and let what the fish had mentioned waddle through my mind and out. I didn't think about it again. In fact, by the time I hopped on the bus--consumed by my tardiness--all I could think about was lunch and how late I already was.

3

I rang the doorbell twice. My best friend Michael, the one who invited me to his home for lunch, opened the door. He wore a black coat and ridiculous red-dotted shorts. They were probably from the nineties, which was his thing, and I thought they looked rather silly.

"You're late . . . actually, you're more than just late," he said, his voice rose as he checked the wall clock. The tick-tock of the clock made a loud clank each time the second hand swept by the 12. The second hand, in fact, seemed to swirl around the face of the clock too quickly, which I thought, perhaps, Michael's clock was broken.

He staggered out of the doorway to let me in. Probably drunk off wine-a habit he refused to break-so seeing him drunk in the doorway at this hour was no surprise.

"Damn bus was an hour late, some kind of accident. But better late than never," I replied as I entered the apartment.

His apartment was on the 28th floor overlooking the entire mid-city and it was such a treat to visit him every once in a while because the view made everything spectacular. His place was a wall-to-wall party with a potpourri of characters. There was Luis, he was the one-up guy, and the one disliked the most. I wasn't sure why he was always invited. Michael didn't like him to begin with. Of course, Luis sat alone. Like I said, no one liked spending time with him. He always said the wrong thing at the wrong time to the wrong person.

To my right were Claire and Daisy. They sat near the entrance, each with a glass of wine. They were both in their twenties and beautiful. Daisy was more attractive and I think Michael wanted to sleep with her, or perhaps, he had slept with her, which is why she was here to begin with. Claire followed Daisy as if her job was to watchout for her. After all, she was a big sister-like role model for Daisy, and Claire always saved her from herself, at least, most of the time.

BEAUTIFUL AND DAMNED

Coming out of the restroom was Joe. He was the spirit of the room. Everywhere he went, he was the life of the party. He affected all of us in a way that none of us could understand. Caring and sweet, he was always looking for the best in people.

On the balcony were Carlos, Ethan, and Ethan's sister Erika. Ethan and Carlos were the enforcers of the group--the ones who protected all of us. Erika, being Ethan's older sister, was the mature one. She was college educated and brilliant. If you spoke to her about life, you would question your own existence by the time she was through.

I went around the apartment and greeted everyone, except Luis. I was still baffled about why he was here to begin with. With a beer in one hand, I headed to the balcony to chat to Ethan. It had been a few weeks since I last saw him. He talked to me about his life and that he felt he should be doing more. But we all felt this way. We all knew we could be doing so much more with our lives and because of this, I believe it was normal to feel as if you didn't know what you were doing or where you were meant to go. No one ever knew. Everyone was kind of finding clues about themselves as they went along.

"It's just sometimes I feel like I'm trapped within myself. Like I have so much to offer, but I just don't know how to get it out. And what's worse? Almost everyone I spend time with, excluding all of you, find a way to drag me down. If only things were back to the days when we were all kids. Things were always so simple back then." Ethan looked out at the view.

I stood right beside him, caught in deep thought. I felt bad for Ethan. All his life, he fought hard to be liked, to be accepted, but then again, didn't we all? Didn't we all just want to belong to a certain group or a certain class? Maybe what he felt wasn't so tragic. Maybe it was just a phase, one we all go through, eventually.

"I think you're right where you should be," I said thoughtfully. "Everyone feels like this at some point or maybe even all the time. I think it's normal. I never know what I'm doing, which is funny because people come to me for help or advice. I'm the go-to guy, but the reality is, I don't know what I'm doing myself."

"Yeah, I hear you," said Ethan as Carlos and Erika began to laugh. We both turned our heads toward their direction.

"What are you guys laughing about?" Ethan asked as he took a gulp from his beer.

"Nothing, just some randomness," said Erika as she lifted a cigarette from a little green ashtray. Carlos just looked at us and smiled.

41

I turned back to continue my conversation, but Ethan had vanished. I thought this was odd because I would have seen him walk back in.

"Erika, where did Ethan go?"

"Ethan? Who's Ethan?" she said.

"Yeah, right," I said sarcastically.

"Are you ok there, Adrian? You don't look so well," said Carlos as he sat in front of Erika with his feet dangling from a chair.

Okay, amusing. They were all playing a joke. It wouldn't be the first time.

"What do you mean who is he? C'mon guys, stop playing. Where's Ethan?" I said as I opened the balcony door. There was no way he could have passed by me. It was a remarkably heavy door that squeaked when opened or closed. I would have heard the door open.

"I'll find him myself," I said as I went into the apartment. The first person I ran into was Luis, who was still alone. I *still* wondered why the hell he was here. I preferred not to deal with him, but I had no choice. Maybe he'd seen Ethan. I went up to him nonchalantly as if I hadn't purposely ignored him when I first arrived.

"Oh Luis, I didn't know you were here. How are you?" I asked.

"I'm good," he replied. "Is it true you've got a thing for that Pederson girl?"

Shit! Where'd he hear that? And what made him think that my business was his? Like I said: wrong thing, wrong time, wrong person. I ignored his nosy question. "Hey, um, by any chance did you see Ethan pass by here?"

"Who's Ethan? I don't think I've met him," he said as he looked the other way. He seemed uninterested in talking to me if I wasn't going to give him the details about Lori Pederson. I hid my frown and kept my mouth neutral.

I had no idea what was going on. Who included him in the joke?

I walked up to Joe and asked him the same question.

"Who's Ethan?" he said, his brow furrowed.

Daisy and Claire gave me the same reply. I asked Michael. No luck. No one knew Ethan. I mean seriously. No one had any idea who I was talking about. It was as if he had been erased from everyone's memory.

Panic sat on my shoulder like a persuasive demon but
I played it calm and no one noticed. I walked into the
kitchen, opened the refrigerator, grabbed another beer
and leaned against the wall that faced the balcony.
Everyone seemed the same. No one seemed to be worried.
No one seemed to care. It was as if everyone had
stepped behind a veil. What the hell was going on? I
drank the entire beer in one take. I walked back to the
refrigerator and grabbed another. I drank it in one
shot. Yes. I used alcohol to relax; sometimes it was my
only escape. I did a quick search of the apartment. No
Ethan. Had he gone for more beer? I grabbed another
brew and asked my friends about Ethan once again. Worry
crossed their faces. They weren't messing with me, for
no one knew who Ethan was and no one cared about the
things I was asking.

4

I was already a little disoriented. I had asked
everyone several times if they had seen Ethan and got
the same results. No one knew who he was. I dug into my
phone and tried to find a photo of him but all the
photos were gone or he was missing from the picture. It
was as if he no longer existed, as if he'd never been
born. Everything about him had been stolen and no one
but me had any memories of who he was. I didn't want to
give up on him that easily. I even closed my eyes
tightly and tried to wake myself up. After all, this
felt like a terrible nightmare, one of those late-for-

work-can't-make-a-call dreams that won't stop. I got up
from the sofa to go to the restroom to rinse my face
with cold-water while everyone stayed in the living
room talking. As I walked past my friends, Daisy got up
and smiled at me.

"Where are you going?" she asked as she placed her
hand on my shoulder. Her hand felt as if she wore a
frozen glove. I automatically jerked back.

"I'm going to the restroom," I said offering her an
awkward smile. I glanced back at Daisy as if I was
running away from her, but I wasn't. I just really had
to clear my thoughts and recollect myself. You know,
snap myself back to reality.

I went in the restroom, locked the door and faced
the mirror. There was something different about my
face. I knew it was me but I didn't look like me. Well,
I did but I didn't. Something was off. I turned on the
faucet and cupped cold water onto my face. I gripped
the sink with both hands and I tried to stay quiet in
my mind, but out of nowhere that anxiety-laden techno
music from earlier came to me. Wasn't the bus stop
where things started to change?

"Adrian, are you done? I really have to go!" It was
Claire; her breathless voice was easily recognizable.

"Yeah, um, give me a second. I'll be right out," I
shook my head and grabbed the towel that hung on the

wall. I rubbed my face dry, took another look at myself, inhaled, and opened the door. Claire stood in front of the door and hurried past me as she pushed me out of the restroom. She locked the door and I immediately heard the toilet seat slam.

I walked into the living room and sat on the couch next to Michael. He didn't say a word. His focus was on the ceiling. Zoned out. So drunk he wasn't saying anything and I didn't say anything either. I just sat there while Luis stared at the wall; Erika and Carlos were still outside. Joe and Daisy were by the kitchen and Claire was in the restroom. And Ethan? He simply had gone missing. I tried to ignore it and everything else that was happening, but something inside of me kept pushing. Something wanted to know what happened. I mean it's not every day that something like this occurs, and today, in general, had been such a strange day to begin with—starting with my alarm not going off.

5

Michael was here, but he wasn't here. His mind and probably even his soul were off to some far out place. I knew this because every time he got drunk his eyes spaced out and his body stiffened. It was almost as if he would pass into the next reality to come back stronger and wiser each time.

Michael raised his hand without saying a word. He kept glaring at the ceiling. His eyes rolled back and he pointed toward his bedroom. It was closed, no one was ever allowed in his bedroom, especially when he had people over. I looked at him and then his bedroom door, I looked at him again and then, the door for the second time. His hand waved me to go as if he wanted me to enter his bedroom. I didn't say a word as I stood up. Maybe Ethan was hiding there and this was all some cruel joke. I walked to the hallway while Claire was still in the restroom, on her phone--and I say this because it sounded like she was playing a video game. I walked by the restroom and took a few steps in front of his bedroom door. I looked back at Michael and his hand waved me in for the second time. I opened the door and went inside. I left the door slightly opened.

To my surprise, there was a girl and a guy sitting on the bed. I couldn't see their faces because they were looking out the window. I stood behind them and didn't make a sound. They weren't moving; they sat there like heavy statues. I took a look at their faces and to my surprise it was Rayne and the techno kid, sitting there, the same way they were sitting while we all were waiting for the bus earlier. I sat next to Rayne. She didn't look at me. The techno kid ignored me, as well.

"Rayne? What are you doing here?" I whispered.

"What does it look like I'm doing? I'm waiting," she said as she continued to stare out the window. Her legs were crossed and her hands rested on her lap. There was no suitcase or briefcase as before. It was just the both of them and nothing else.

"Rayne, but you're in a room. What are you waiting for in here?" She turned my way and gave me a disgusted look.

"I'm waiting for the bus. The same way you're waiting for the bus. Stop asking such stupid questions."

"How could you possibly be waiting for a bus in someone's bedroom, Rayne? You're not making any sense. Why are you in Michael's house? Why are you in his room? You don't even know him. None of you do. I would have met you sooner if you did," I said.

"Maybe this makes perfect sense and you're the one not making any sense. I'm waiting for a bus and who is to say this is a room? Who is to say whom I don't know and whom I do? And who is to say who Michael is? Maybe I am Michael, maybe you're Michael and maybe we are all in your very *own* room. The world is filled with lies and everything we know is part of that lie," she said as she gazed back out the window.

"Besides, I was here first. I've been waiting here for an hour. So my question to you is, what are *you* doing here?" She glanced at me, winked, and her focus went straight back to the window. The techno kid didn't say a word. This was far too weird. Was I losing my mind? Had I already lost it? I felt as if I had taken a dive into the deep end. I stomped out of the room and slammed it shut. Three steps and I looked at the couch. Michael was gone; in fact, no one was left in the apartment. And then, I went back to Michael's bedroom and it, too, was empty. What the hell?

I walked towards the couch and began to think and think and think. I thought what if I went outside and got some help. Yes, that's it, that's the perfect idea! I got up from the couch and walked towards the door. I unlocked it and pulled it open but it was sealed shut. I struggled with it but it was no use. This door wasn't going to open.

I sat down on the couch. I couldn't believe what was happening. First, Ethan disappeared, then, I find Rayne and techno kid in the room, and then my entire affiliation is gone as if they'd all fallen off the face of the earth. I tried to remain calm. I concentrated on coming up with a plan. I closed my eyes and when I opened them, I noticed something drifting from the ceiling. I couldn't tell what it was, but it was gently swinging itself downward in a spiral motion.

And then I clearly saw it. It was a spider, the size of a quarter. It hung right in front of me.

"Adrian! Adrian! You've got to help me!" said the spider with a squeaky little voice.

"Wha . . . ex . . . cuse me?" I stuttered. My tongue pressed upon the roof of my mouth and my hands grasped each other.

"Adrian, it's me. Ethan. What the hell is going on?"

"Ethan? How do I know you're Ethan?" I said knowing that this for sure was a dream. I raise my hand to tear the web.

"Wait!" It screamed. "In the third grade, you and I became spit brothers. Remember? And we swore not to tell anyone because the spit fell all over our faces. Remember?" he said as his eight legs dangled from his web. And that was true, Ethan and I had become spit brothers in the third grade and there was no way anyone else would have ever known this.

"Ethan? What the hell is going on, man? You're a goddamn spider!!!"

"I know! What the hell!"

"But how? How could all of this happen?" I was hysterical and so was he.

"I don't know but yesterday I saved a kitten from getting run over. I stopped in the middle of the street and almost got myself killed, but you know me, I had to save it. Then, something weird happened."

"A lot of strange things have been happening lately, Ethan--"

"And then, the kitten spoke and said it was a djinn, and it wanted to grant me a wish for saving it. I didn't know what to do. I'm thinking, *a talking kitten*, no way. And what the hell is a djinn? I took it to the animal shelter and let them deal with the kitten. After that, well, the next day, strange things started happening and now I'm a spider. Help me!"

"I just had the same thing happen to me. I saved a red fish and it made me the same offer. Now, I'm trapped in a lucid nightmare, and you're a spider, and everyone is missing, and these two other people I met at the bus stop were in Michael's room waiting for the bus to arrive.I mean a bus, can you believe that? And for me, it all just started about two hours ago. I don't know what to do. I'm trapped in Michael's apartment, I mean *we*, and the door is sealed shut. We need to get help."

"Let me think; there has to be a way out. Someone needs to help us," said Ethan as he continued to hang. We stayed silent for a moment. Thinking.

"I got it! Once we find a way out, we can see this gypsy lady my mom sees. Shoot, I can't remember her

name, but she's into black magic and things like this.
Perhaps, if we go to her, she can help get us out of
this, whatever this is."

The plan sounded good enough. All we had to do was
come up with a way to get out.

"I got it," said Ethan.

"What if you flush me down the toilet? I'll work my
way into the plumbing and exit at a sewer. There must
be a place where it all goes. You know what I mean?"

As Ethan said that, I heard the toilet flush, and
someone in the restroom turned the faucet on. *I checked
the bathroom minutes before and no one was there.*
Scared, I froze. The bathroom door opened and out
walked Claire, drying her hands with a paper towel.

"Geez, where did everybody go?" she said with a
sassy voice. She walked directly toward me.

"Oh my! A spider!" she yelled as both of her hands
slammed against each other.

"Oh my fucking god! You killed Ethan!!! You just
killed Ethan!!!"

"What?" she said, her face confused and unsure of
what it was I was saying.

My eyes darted towards the paper towel as his lifeless little body smeared it. I ran straight past her and locked myself shut into the restroom. Claire, being the motherly figure she was, ran behind me but she didn't make it in. She kept knocking on the restroom door. Banging on it like a drum. The clamor just made me more uneasy. I headed to the window but slid on the bathroom rug and conked my head on the tub.

Pounding the door, Claire wouldn't let up.

"Adrian, open the door! Stop kidding around! Where is everyone? I'm scared, let me in!" she kept saying this over and over as I began to feel ill to my stomach. I wanted to throw up but nothing came out and then, I whispered to myself as Claire kept banging on the door.

"I don't know what is going on. The world has gone upside down. People are missing, my best friends are missing. I... I just don't know what to do... I just wish none of this was happening right now."

And then... a loud pop went off. It sounded like a light bulb being dropped and I was back where I started again.

6

I didn't drive. Not because I didn't have a car or a license but because I didn't like the idea of being inside a box with four wheels, surrounded by other people trapped in other boxes with other four wheels. Because of this, I took the train, the bus, or rode my bicycle whenever I needed to. Walking was a last resort. It was worse than driving. One of my best friends got himself killed walking. He was on the sidewalk when a car accidentally hit him. I guess, this was why I didn't like cars or walking.

I was already late. My friend had invited me to have lunch with him and a handful of our friends. I walked down 8th and Flagler Street to the bus stop, right in front of the university. I had been waiting at the bus stop for nearly 15 minutes. Of course, it felt longer. When you had to wait for over 10 minutes for anything, the minutes would drag.

I was supposed to be there at noon. Being late makes me panicky, and having to wait, while being late, was worse. It wasn't in my character to be late and yet, I had forgotten about this get-together and only remembered it about 30 minutes ago.

To my surprise, there was no one sitting here with me and I found that to be odd. Every time I passed this stop, it was always filled with people. I wondered why

it was so empty today, on a Tuesday, about a quarter
past noon. There was no sunshine. No city noise. No
cars passing by. It didn't feel like an ordinary day.
Something was different and forgetting a lunch date was
the first sign. Strange things could happen when you
are alone and by that, I mean anything could happen
when you're alone. But it's not like I was expecting a
tornado to drift me into Oz. No, not that, although
that would be a marvelous story to tell.

Time passed and finally, a student arrived. I could
tell he was a student by his book-bag and he limped as
he pulled a suitcase. Maybe it wasn't a suitcase; I'm
not sure. It looked as if he had a musical instrument
in there. When he got to the bus stop, he just dropped
everything as if it were dead weight, something of no
use to him. He sighed. He was a pretty big guy, by that
I mean heavy. He was maybe about 6" 1', 300, maybe even
400 pounds. He wore old headphones and obnoxiously loud
techno music blasted from them. God, it was awful. I
don't understand how anyone could develop such a taste
for that kind of music. He looked at me and didn't say
a word. I glanced back and quickly turned away, minding
my own business. The last thing I needed was small
talk. I hated small talk; it cheapened everything.

"You got a light?" the kid asked as this awful scent
of old earth and dry skin radiated from his clothes. He
smelled terrible; I wasn't sure how I didn't catch that
sooner.

"Uh no, I don't smoke, sorry," I replied as I tucked both of my feet beneath the bench.

"Well, that's good. Smoking can kill you," he said.

What terrible humor, I thought. *A smoker telling a non-smoker not to smoke because smoking could potentially kill you*? How do you detach yourself from that? This guy made no sense whatsoever, but that in itself interested me. I took a leap and began to talk to him and it was something I normally didn't do.

"So, what are you listening to?"

"Prodigy," he said as his head rocked back and forth. I thought it was rather strange the way his head bobbed like it was attached to a spring.

"Wow, I haven't heard Prodigy in forever."

"Yeah, they're awesome," he said as he continued to bebop. I didn't know what to think of this guy.

Suddenly, he grabbed his book bag and searched through it.

"I got one!" he shouted in victory as if he had just won a contest.

"Got what?"

"Some matches," he said as he took an old box of matches out and lit the cigarette up.

"This makes waiting for the bus so much easier." He took a few tokes and blew the smoke in the other direction. Even so, the wind slowly swept it toward my face and I held my breath until it passed.

A girl walked toward the bus stop carrying a briefcase. She was about 5'2", maybe around 100 pounds, and had enchanting brown hair with auburn streaks. The way she walked made it difficult not to notice her sinewy legs. Once she was close enough, I could see her gray eyes that looked like the moon when it was full.

"Hey," said the guy with the techno music as she sat on the edge of the bench, to my left.

"Hi," she said with a shy smile. She placed the briefcase on the ground and shoved a handful of papers into the side pocket.

"Hi, I'm Adrian." I extended my hand to greet her. This was something I normally didn't do, but like I said, I was panicky, and being so can make you do things, unexpected things.

"Hi Adrian, I'm Rayne," she said, her voice like rose petals, soft and bouncy.

I thought that was an unusual name. I mean, really, what kind of parent would name their child Rain? I had never heard of such a name. I mean, it didn't sound awful, no, not at all, but it was rather left-sided. She must have had it bad in grade school. I could instantly think of a million different ways to make fun of her name.

The techno kid pulled a little brown box from his suitcase. He opened it to reveal a pile of little white squares of candy.

"Does anyone want some bubble gum?" He extended his arm toward Rayne and me. We looked at each other for a moment--I think because it was so random, the way the techno kid asked. You know, we've all heard about taking candy from strangers, besides that, it was such an awkward thing to ask.

"It's special gum; it's not from around here," he insisted. I thought about it but not much. It was a piece of gum: nothing more, nothing less.

"Okay, I'll have one." I reached into the small wooden box for a piece. Rayne did the same.

We continued to talk about school, politics, sports, music and several other things. It made the wait bearable. Plus, the more time I spent with these strangers, the more I felt like being late to my friend's lunch wasn't such a bad thing after all.

7

"Help me" a loud voice emerged. It was coming from a dumpster near the lake in front of the university. I looked around and asked Rayne if she had heard anything.

"Did you hear anything? Like someone yelling in distress?"

"No, I don't hear anyone." She went back to her book.

"Help me . . . Someone, please save me. It's going eat me!" The voice continued. I wanted to see what it was, but something inside of me told me not to go. Something inside of me was pulling me away from it. The voice kept begging its desperate plea again and again and again. And it lasted for well over half an hour. Until, suddenly, the voice just stopped.

By the time my bus came, I was alone. Rayne had jumped on her bus and so did the techno kid. They were all going on different routes. I didn't get Rayne's number, although, I should have had asked her for it. I liked her; she made me feel good inside.

About half way into my route I grabbed my cell phone from my pocket and I had several missed calls and text messages, all from the bunch of friends who awaited my arrival. I was, after all, always on time. Most of the messages asked if I was even coming and some were worried because I was so late.

I was about two blocks from my stop when an older man entered the bus. He carried a camouflage bag and wore an old fisherman's hat on his head. His beard passed the midsection of his torso. He stood by the edge of the entrance and looked for a seat from afar. Soon after, he walked through the crowd, made his way to my aisle, and sat next to me. He didn't say a word-- didn't even thank me for moving my belongings to make room for him to sit. I thought it was rude but didn't make much of it. I just minded my own business and was attentive to my stop.

As I waited, the old man shuffled through his bag and pulled out a black book with a little red fish on the cover. The title said *Djinns*. I wasn't sure what a djinn was, but something familiar came to me like a broken memory. I sunk within a pool of unknowns. I wasn't sure what it was or what it meant, but something was pleading for me to find out. This suspicious curiosity rode. The image of the little red fish on the cover seemed so familiar, like it was lodged somewhere in my memory. Yet, I knew I had never seen such an image. I glanced at the man and tapped his shoulder.

"What's that book about, mister?" I asked.

He grabbed the book and placed it on his lap. He looked as if he had gone through something terrible in his life. His face was racked with sadness as his eyes began to water and his jaw shifted tight.

"This here book is something you don't want to know," the man said as he quickly placed the book back into his bag.

I sat there stunned at his blatant rudeness. Before I could say anything, a quarter-sized black spider crawled out of his sleeve and went straight into his bag. The man took one good look at me as if he wanted to remember me forever and then he vanished right in front of my eyes.

Before my stop even came, I got off the bus as quickly as I could, I ran out in terror without looking behind me and I swear, I never went back to that bus stop again.

BEAUTIFUL AND DAMNED

She didn't need to be loved,
she just needed someone
to understand her and tell her
how everything was going to be okay.

I NEVER FORGOT YOU

1

Scarlett and Hector had been together for over a decade, 14 years to be exact-a high school friendship destined never to end. Scarlett, who was slightly older, always wanted more. She knew there was something greater out in the world. She never blamed Hector for staying stuck in their hometown, but she did feel a scorching void--one she was never able to fill.

They met in grade school. Hector was always isolated and if it weren't for grade school, he would have never met Scarlett. He was, at times, picked on by his peers and sometimes pushed to his limit, but ultimately, he was always in good spirits.

One day during grade school, he sat out back at the picnic tables during a sweltering day. No one was out and no one was around him. Hector was alone and he always felt alone, but not because of this, but because of his life in general. Scarlett, on the other hand, always had friends around her and as she grew up, more people were attracted to her. Not in a physical manner,

although she was ambiguously beautiful, but in a
spiritual way. People flocked to her. She had good
energy and was fun and joyous to be around.

That day, she saw Hector all alone, sitting out back
with his lunch completed. She did something she
normally wouldn't have done. She walked up to Hector
and sat beside him. Hector managed to see her from the
corner of his eye but being to himself, he didn't say a
word. His lips tightened together and he clamped his
hands together. He wasn't sure what was going on.

"What's wrong with you?" said 10-year-old Scarlett.
She placed her hands on the table as if it were a
piano, her fingers tapping an imaginary song.

Hector hesitated, he wanted to say something, but he
didn't know what. It had been a longtime since someone
showed interest in him.

"Nothing is wrong with me," Hector replied flatly.
He avoided eye contact. Nervous, he could barely open
his mouth to say more words.

"The other kids think you're weird. So there must be
something wrong with you," Scarlett said.

Hector sighed faintly and his shoulders slightly
hunched.

"Maybe there *is* something wrong with me," he said, gloom coating every word.

"Why?" said Scarlett, her butterfly barrettes sparkling in the sun.

"Because I have a hard time making friends and, if you haven't noticed, no one pays attention to me." And it was true. All his life, he had been treated as if he didn't exist, as if he was trapped in a very faraway place-a place that consumed the darkness and very little light escaped to. He felt like he was in this place because no one ever noticed him, no one ever actually bothered to ask him his name. He was invisible to most, if not all. Even his teachers ignored him. He was that easy to forget and that hard to remember. He felt like a stranger within himself to the point that every morning he wasn't even sure who stared back at him from the mirror.

His gaze fell to the ground. He didn't want to be questioned anymore by Scarlett. He didn't know where else to go but the depths of himself. He didn't say another word and that was something he often did. He would run away from the other children because he felt too out of place. He'd come to accept that he just didn't belong.

"Maybe you're not so weird. Maybe you're just misunderstood," the 10-year-old said to Hector with a smile. She gently placed her left hand over Hector's hand. Her softness slowly spread throughout his body. He smiled back and for once, he felt as if someone had finally discovered him. He felt a pulse coming from the floor of his soul and it lifted him like a balloon elevating towards the sky. It felt like a breath of fresh air--one he had been waiting for all his life and soon after, they were inseparable.

They did everything together. They studied together. They laughed together and as time flew by, their innocence flourished and they became best friends. But often, like most friendships, they soon enough become more.

By the time the two went to high school, things changed. Hector came out of his shell and was suddenly popular. Scarlett became more isolated and into herself and her studies. But none of that changed the bond between them, for as they grew, so did their attraction to one another.

When Hector finally had the courage to ask Scarlett to be more than just friends, he didn't have a cent to his name, let alone anything else to offer. Scarlett was 18 when Hector revealed what he felt for her and it was no surprise that she, too, felt the very same way. And just like that, they became closer--and the world never bothered to drift them apart as their love slowly stemmed out of the burning earth like the last tree the world was meant to see.

Together they experienced many things. They shared their first date, shared their first kiss, and eventually shared love. They both knew they had the capacity to love but never thought their hearts could reach such depths. To Scarlett and Hector, there was no life, no world, no reason of being, and no other person, that is, if it didn't involve them both. The two were inseparable and it went on like this for several years. Together they had so much more. It was as if they had a secret pact, one no one ever understood. But as they got older, a crack sprouted within the life they created for themselves. The crack grew deeper as the days accumulated and the void within Scarlett and the distance within Hector took root. And now they found each other in a predicament, a real problem, and it was one they could have never imagined for themselves.

2

On the second day of February, Hector had just got home from work. He worked as a computer technician for a local office. He didn't learn how to fix computers in trade school or the university; it was just something he picked up from watching his engineer friends. He was a quick learner and usually, if he put his mind into something, he learned it with such precision and talent.

BEAUTIFUL AND DAMNED

It was 8:32 p.m. and Scarlett had finished cooking dinner while Hector was in the shower. Scarlett had gone to a university to become a registered nurse. She worked three days a week doing 12-hour shifts. On her days off, she would stay home and clean. But something inside of her always told her to do more. At times, especially when she was alone, she would sit for hours. She couldn't help but wonder, what if she had never sat by Hector that one day in grade school? What if she had ignored him like all the other children did? Those same questions had been lodged in her mind for years.

It had been 14 years and not to say those 14 years were terrible, because they weren't, but to say something along the lines of "what if we had never met?" and "how different would our lives be?" or "where would I be? In what country? In what city?" She did love Hector more than anything, but like all people, she always questioned her station in life and always wondered if she did deserve more.

By the time they went to bed, it was well past midnight. Together in a king sized bed, in a small bedroom, in a small apartment; they laid flat on the mattress. Hector was with his shirt off because they were trying to save money and did so by shutting off the air conditioner every other night. That helped them cut their monthly bills in half.

The room was reasonably warm. Hector turned over and looked at Scarlett with a gentle stare. She turned off her nightstand lamp and turned the night-light on. The room was now dark, their faces barely visible as night crawled across the sky.

Scarlett bounced onto the bed as she grabbed her covers and looked at Hector's silhouette. He placed his palm on her shoulder and moved it in swirls. He would do so every time he wanted to talk. Scarlett already knew there was something on his mind, even though he hadn't said a word.

"Do you remember how we first met?" he asked.

"Of course, I do. There's no way I could forget it. You were so out of place. You stood out, you know?" she replied.

Hector laughed, it was almost a silent laughter, the kind you would do when you didn't want anyone to hear you.

"Why did you do it? I mean, what made you talk to me that day? I was such a peculiar kid. No one ever paid any attention to me, but you--for some odd reason did. How come? Was it a dare of some sort? Perhaps, a joke that didn't go as expected? Do you ever wonder what if that never happened? How different our lives would be? Does that ever cross your mind?" said Hector as he continued to glide his palm over her shoulder.

Scarlett went silent for a few moments. She didn't know where Hector was going with this conversation. She didn't want to expect anything, especially when she, too, now and then, would ask herself the same question. And she would always feel bad because she never mentioned this to Hector. She just let it dwell deeply within the closets of her heart.

"Why are you asking me such a thing? Aren't you happy we're together? This is the way our lives are supposed to be. This is the way it turned out. And I can't explain what it was. I just saw you and something within you called out to me--like an inaudible sound that only my ears could have interpreted. It was something so loud I couldn't ignore it. You had that--"

Hector jumped in before she could finish her sentence.

"I *had* that? What's that supposed to mean? What do you mean by had?" Hector asked.

Scarlett felt as if he was trying to force something out of her, something like an argument. She could feel his energy bouncing off the wall and slamming straight into the center of her chest. This wasn't the first time something like this had manifested. She thought maybe Hector had a bad day at work and was taking it out on her, which was unacceptable but realistic, and she understood that.

"You didn't let me finish, I didn't mean it like that," Scarlett replied, but she wasn't sure how she meant it. In fact, she wasn't even sure how those words found their place on the edge of her tongue. She did love Hector; there was no denying that. But--and there was always a but--when it came to things like this, to matters of the heart. . . if your heart wasn't truly there, but it was, but it wasn't, it's hard to know how things will go from one day to the next. And maybe hers had wandered away because it did that at times, but she never made a fuss about it. Sometimes she would be as happy as a bee drunk on pollen, and then, sometimes, although it was rare, she wanted to get away, start over, meet new people and go to different places. And perhaps, because of that, she wasn't content with her life, but she didn't blame Hector--she blamed all these feelings on herself.

They stayed silent momentarily as if they hadn't the courage to continue, but they did. This conversation was waiting to surface, waiting for it to be lifted into the air and inhaled. It had been brewing for several years now, especially in the heart of Scarlett. She just didn't know how to put her feelings into words and there were no words really. There was no easy way to express these things because these types of conversations just happen, they just are. There was no pre-planned way to express this, and even if there were, it would never come out the way you expected. Life wasn't that easy.

"We said we would always be honest with each other, didn't we Scarlett? We said there would never be a lie between us. Right?"

"Yes, I remember, and I have always kept my promise," Scarlett said as she nodded her head.

Hector lifted his palm from her shoulder and turned his back into the mattress as he faced the ceiling above him. Scarlett, too, did the same. She didn't know where this conversation was going, but she had an idea. Everything started with an idea and it didn't matter how big or how small, every idea had an impact, a life-changing and shifting moment, and that was what led you or changed your direction--no matter where you were meant to go. In an instant, an idea could change everything, and they both understood this. And her idea of wanting more had been lingering far too heavily to ignore. It was always above her like a dark cloud-- reminding her that perhaps, she wasn't living her life the way she had envisioned as a little girl.

"I don't know what makes me happy anymore." Hector didn't move as his lips softly touched. He couldn't move after that, for it was something he had been holding in for a long time. As he released these words, these feelings, something inside him fractured into a thousand little pieces. And there was nothing he could do about that.

"By that," Hector explained, "I mean, I don't know
if you make me happy anymore. I don't know if we make
each other happy. I mean, there's no excitement, no
fire, no desire, not anything that makes us, well, me,
feel like that person you fell in love with. And every
night I feel terrible about the way I feel--like I'm
stranded on an island and all I can see is you, flying
above me, ignoring me. Leaving me behind as I wave for
your help. And what's worse, sometimes I feel as if I'm
okay with that. I'm okay with being alone; being lost
out at sea on an undisclosed island and never finding
my way back home. Am I that horrible of a person to
feel this way?" Hector's voice cracked a little and a
stream of tears fell from his eyes--onto his pillow. He
felt numb and cold as if he lay on a bed of ice.

Scarlett knew what to say, but her words clung to
the back of her throat as if they were too much for the
outside world, and the world wasn't ready to catch them
as they plunged out of her mouth.

"I know how you feel," she whispered.

Hector didn't say a word.

"I know how you feel, Hector, because I feel the
same way. There are nights when I feel like I don't
know myself anymore. There are nights when I look at
myself in the mirror and wonder how could my life have
turned out this way? How could I have let this happen
and it's not because of you, it's because of me. I have

always felt something, that is . . . . I have always had
this void, and some days when I wake up in the morning,
I am lost in it. I am falling into a bottomless pit of
nothingness," Scarlett said as she sobbed. Her tears
were filled with honesty and truth. It was the only way
she could have ever expressed all that she had been
feeling for far too long.

Hector, too, sobbed. He wanted to grab her and
comfort her, but he didn't have it in him. He just laid
there as he reflected on all the years they had spent
together. Her tears, too, were a reflection of a life
filled with love, both whole and broken, but it was, in
fact, love. Drops of sadness began to fall from his
eyes again, staining his face as they fell. Each tear
was a moment they had spent together, a memory that he
held on to. He didn't know why he felt this way and he
wasn't sure if it was the right thing to say, but it
had been eating away at his laughter for several years
now. If this was the moment, then this was it. He
wanted to seize it, no matter what.

"So what happens now?" Hector asked as if Scarlett
had the answer.

Scarlett continued to sob. She couldn't believe what
she had spluttered. *Was this really happening*? She
thought to herself as the dark cloud above her
thundered. She felt weightless, like a feather caught
in a storm.

"I don't know." That was the best answer she could
have given Hector. That was the only thing that was
secure. She didn't know. Was anyone supposed to know?
One thing was certain, whatever lay on the other side
of their lives was bound to be something they both
needed and something that would arrive in the form of
all things unexpected.

They couldn't sleep the rest of the night. They just
lay there, as if life was slowly being pulled out of
them, like a thin yarn attached to the corners of their
souls. They didn't talk, they were silent with each
other and with themselves, and they continued to
breathe throughout the night, with new wounds and a
handful of possibilities. They kept wide-awake and all
they could think of was what they had just said.

3

It had been three years since Scarlett had seen
Hector. Three long, slow years and within those years,
Scarlett had found the courage to do all the things she
dreamed of. She traveled the world, went to all the
places she had hoped to see and lived every second the
way she wanted to. She was enthusiastic about her life
and she always saw everything with incredible color and
wonder. She even grew different in appearance and
changed her entire outlook on things. She was now head
nurse and was able to have a little more clout at work.

Sometime, within the last three years, Scarlett had even found a new flame. He was a young man named Julian. They had met one night when she was at a charity event in Los Angeles. He was an educated man of fair build. His hobbies were similar to Scarlett's. He was intrigued by his own curiosity and lived his life as if it was an adventure and, because of this, Scarlett couldn't deny him. He was everything she wasn't and she was everything he wanted to be. The spark between them set the sky on fire and buried all regret beneath their feet. She was in love and it was not partially, it was not broken or confusing. It was everything she wanted and more. It made all the stars come together and made everything she had been holding within clear. She understood how nothing was ever perfect, but for some odd reason, she couldn't have been happier. Her void, the one she had since the beginning of it all, was nothing more but a speck, something she couldn't feel anymore. It was something unrecognizable. She was glad she couldn't remember how the void felt, how she felt before, but something in the back of her head always nagged at her. It was like a vault--one that had been locked with the key hidden in the depths of her heart. But it opened from time to time and when it did, she thought of Hector.

4

It was the eighth of March and Scarlett was planning where to celebrate her birthday. Her birthday was right around the corner; it was two days from now and she was turning 35. Every year she planned at the very last minute and every year she celebrated it randomly. This year, like all years, she had an idea, but as usual, they never went accordingly.

Scarlett waited for her friend to meet her for dinner. This was how she planned most of her birthdays: with good company, good food, and good wine. It was almost 8 p. m. and she was already on her second glass of red wine.

A vibration stirred her thigh. She grabbed her phone; a text message from Grace had come in:

"I'm running late. There is so much traffic, it's awful. See you soon. XOXO."

Grace was her best friend. She was always there for Scarlett and with each year that passed, the two became closer. They were like sisters. Sometimes they didn't see eye to eye, but no matter what the outcome, the two would always fly back home. Grace was Scarlett's support, her wall, her protector, and in the end, she always knew what was best for her. And Scarlett needed that at times; she needed a strong woman with a solid character to pull her out of the shadows. She always thought if it wasn't for Grace, the split between her and Hector would have dragged her to the pits of hell and left her there to burn. In other words, Grace saved Scarlett and Grace had become more than just another shoulder to lean on during her times of shade. She had become her savior and for that, Scarlett was always grateful.

A finger tapped Scarlett's shoulder; it was Grace. She had finally arrived.

"I made it, dear," said Grace as she leaned toward Scarlett and stamped her cheek with a kiss.

"You started without me?" Grace scanned the table, which was filled with two empty wine glasses and a few hors d'oeuvres. Scarlett had taken the liberty of ordering.

"What are you drinking?" said Grace.

"Cabernet Sauvignon and thank you for meeting me last minute."

"Don't mention it. You know I'll always be here for you, no matter what."

"So let's get started. My birthday is two nights away and we haven't the slightest clue on what we're doing," said Scarlett enthusiastically.

Scarlett didn't know that Julian and Grace had already planned her entire birthday. They had been planning it for months and Grace had only agreed to meet with Scarlett to distract her from planning it

herself. Grace had been diverting Scarlett's attention
for the past four weeks. A surprise party had been
planned and everyone was already invited. It was going
to be spectacular and memorable.

The rest of the evening, Scarlett kept going back to
the idea of a party and never did she notice how Grace
would retract the subject and dive into something else.
Whenever she brought it up, Grace would order more
drinks and guide the conversation elsewhere. And they
continued their night with good company, good food, and
good wine.

5

On the day of her birthday, Scarlett took the day
off from work. She woke up a little later than usual
and drove to the city to find an outfit to wear for
later. Still, not having the slightest clue on what she
was bound to do, she took it upon herself to make sure
she looked stunning; she bought a dress that shimmered
like the moon during the rain.

Scarlett walked in and out of shops finding
accessories for the emerald, low-backed, silk dress she
had purchased. She felt good. There was something in
the air, something that made the sun look a little
brighter and the sky a little bluer. As she walked
across the street, she heard someone yell out her name.
She looked back but couldn't tell who it was. The

street was full of people, mostly tourists and city workers that blocked her view. Then, she heard a voice yell out her name again. She looked around and saw a homeless man rushing towards her direction.

"Scarlett! He approached her from the middle of the street. He weaved through the traffic as if it was a maze and he had its blueprint. He hurried toward her. His focus caused him to fall as his foot crashed into the curb. The man fell, got up, and continued to walk toward her. She stood there in shock; she didn't know what was going on and she held her belongings tightly. The homeless man limped toward her until he made a complete stop. He kneeled as he caught his breath.

"Scarlett, is that you?" His voice was breathy and brittle. He looked as if he hadn't slept for days. His hair was knotted and his beard grew in uneven spots. Wearing a grimy tank top and pants too weary to sit at his waist, he stood as he focused his eyes straight to hers.

Scarlett, being Scarlett, didn't know what to say. "Do I know you?" Scarlett murmured as her head slightly flinched. His stench caused her nose to crinkle and she took a few subtle steps back.

"Scarlett, is it really you?" said the homeless man as he took a few subtle steps forward.

"I don't think we've met before, sir," Scarlett
replied with an uncomfortable look on her face.

"Scarlett," he sighed he as reached out for her
hand, but she didn't let him touch her. She reacted and
quickly hid her hand from exposure.

"Do I know you?"

"I know it's you. I once knew you and you once knew
me, but that was a lifetime ago. But you, Scarlett,
haven't changed since the first time I saw you in grade
school."

"Hector?" Scarlett whispered, and then she suddenly
began to cry. She never cried with style or grace; she
never knew how to hold her tears in whenever she felt
the need to cry. And she did cry with ferociousness and
intensity as they stood before one another. Her tears
were just the beginning. A violent tremble careened
through her as she looked at Hector--the man she once
loved. Seeing him in such a state broke her from every
direction. Scarlett was thrown into the fire the moment
her eyes connected with Hector's and at that moment,
everything she thought she knew and everything she had
learned in the last three years meant nothing.

"Hector! What happened to you? Why? How?" asked
Scarlett as she swept her hands over her eyes. It was
horrible to see Hector like this. She would have never
imagined him living under these conditions. She wanted

to believe that her eyes deceived her. He looked older, much older, and was barely recognizable, but his eyes were familiar. He had eyes that spoke to people and they were the kind of eyes a child sitting alone at the lunch tables would have. The kind that were easy to remember and hard to forget.

"I started using drugs three years ago and things just got out of hand." Tears welled in his eyes. He didn't know how to make them stop and they didn't. They just kept escaping from the depths of his soul.

Scarlett gently sighed and with soft words she said his name.

"Hector." Her bags fell on the ground.

She couldn't believe her eyes. She wanted to wake up from this terrible, terrible nightmare. She still cared about Hector--loved him. And every so often, she did think about him. She always wondered what had happened to him and where he now lived. She always wanted to know if he was all right or if he was in trouble. She never *really* wanted to let go. She was always willing to work things out in the end.

"You don't have to say anything, Scarlett. I just want to thank you for everything. For the best 14 years of my life. Because of you, I wake up in the morning. Because of you, I try to find hope. I know I won't be like this forever."

Scarlett just stood there. "Hector . . . I . . . ."
she sputtered.

"Believe me, you don't have to say anything. I know,
believe me, I know. Well, I guess this is farewell,
again," said Hector as he bent over to lift her
belongings from the ground and smiled. "It was great
seeing you again, Scarlett." He took one last look at
her. He wanted to hug her, but he didn't, for he had
found himself back when he was a child. He was alone in
the unforgiving darkness.

"Goodbye, Scarlett," said Hector as he began to walk
away. She had lost all sensory abilities; she was
shocked to the very core by what she had seen.

A few seconds later, she walked towards her car,
and, for a third time, she heard Hector yell out her
name from afar.

"Scarlett," he shouted, and she turned around. Her
eyes were drawn to him; they couldn't find anywhere
else to look.

"Happy Birthday," he shouted again. Even from a
distance, his eyes pierced right through her soul. And
in an instant, he became one with the backdrop and
completely vanished into the city like a ghost in the
winter, he was gone.

6

The day after her birthday Scarlett sat in her bedroom and peered out through the balcony. She thought about choices and why things happen the way they are meant to happen. She wondered, what if? What if she had never met Hector? What if she had stayed with him and how different their lives would have been? She thought maybe they could have been happy; maybe they could have worked things out. And every time she thought this throughout the day, she thought how maybe wherever Hector was, if he was thinking the same.

It had been four months since she last saw Hector and not a day passed where she didn't think of him. Almost everything reminded her of him and many times she'd stand where she had last run into him. She wanted to help him. She wanted to be there for him and make sure he was okay. Every day after work, she went to the same spot and waited and waited. Every day she thought about what to say to him and how to help him, but his face never showed. He never came.

Eventually, as time passed, she thought of him less and less, but she never forgot him. She never forgot the boy who was weird and odd, the boy she gave her adolescence to. Soon enough, she stopped going to the last place she had seen him and stopped looking for him, but she never lost hope. She knew how maybe, one day, they were bound to meet again.

About a year later, Scarlett married and several years after that she had two sons of her own, one named Jack and the other, Hector. And she lived her life as she always desired. She lived it full of laughter and full of happiness. She lived it in such a way that she never had to run away from herself. She had found peace and sadly, she never saw Hector again.

BEAUTIFUL AND DAMNED

It hurts because you feel too much,
because you care too much
and because you feel connected
to it all
no matter how far you go.

JACOB

1

There are days when I don't feel like doing anything. Those rainy, lazy kind of days when all you want to do is lay beneath your covers and do nothing. Today is one of those days and the last thing I want to do is go to school. In fact, I know I won't go today. My parents wouldn't notice, either way, I was pretty much in control of my life. They were never around to begin with. They both worked for the same company, which required them to travel about 70% of the time, thus, they were never home, but this time, they were on vacation. Why didn't they take me? I wasn't sure about that one, but it didn't matter, and if they had taken me, I probably wouldn't have cared.

They went to the Bahamas for a week and I had the house to myself. When they'd leave, I'd do as I pleased. I didn't have a bedtime (not like I ever had one) and I stayed awake almost every night. Every time my parents left, I ordered take-out and friends would stay over. You could say I had it pretty good.

BEAUTIFUL AND DAMNED

I was a senior at Gemballa High. It was a prep
school that my parents had forced me to attend. I had
been a student at Gemballa for about two years and I
hated every minute of it. It was 7 a.m. and I was still
wrapped in my pillows and blankets. *Yes, I defiantly
wasn't going to school today*, I thought as I closed my
eyes and sank deeply into a restful sleep.

I woke up at 10 a.m. to an empty house. The sunlight
streamed through the window and the AC blew cold air. I
got up from my bed, brushed my teeth, and walked to the
kitchen to get something to eat, but there was nothing
except cereal. I made myself a bowl and I sat on my
living room couch. I turned the television on, but I
couldn't find anything worth watching. The time passed
slowly, real slow, and that's how it was when I had
nothing to do and during times like these, I would
visit my best comrade, Alex. He was always home. He,
being rebellious, got himself expelled from school
about 9 months ago. Since then, he really didn't do
anything. He wasn't the smartest person I knew but he
was a good friend, perhaps, even a best friend. He was
easy to talk to and he was always there when I needed
him. His humor caught everyone's attention and he
understood people in such a way that he made everyone
around him feel at home. He was full of charm; he had a
good heart. We had been friends for the past several
years. He was one of those people that just grew on me.
The kind you didn't even have to spend too much time to
get to know. He was different, special, and I would

always go to his house whenever I was in need of a good friend. I picked up the phone and gave him a ring.

"Hello?" Said Alex.

"Are you awake? Were you sleeping?" I murmured over the phone.

"Yes, I'm up. How come you're not in school?"

"I didn't feel like going. My parents left on vacation. They're going to be gone for a week."

"Oh, again? It seems like they are gone almost every month. It must be nice to have to house to yourself so often," said Alex.

"I'm going to visit you, okay?" I said as I walked into my bedroom with the phone on my ear. I was looking for a pair of shorts to wear.

"Okay, I'll see you later."

"I'll be there in a few."

"Okay." He hung up the phone.

I grabbed some clothes, a towel, and went straight into the shower. When I was done, I got dressed and did my hair. It was then that I heard a light scratching sound coming from the other side of the wall. It sounded as if a rat was trapped between the frames of the house. There had been a few rat incidents at my parent's house, and every so often, we would have to call the exterminator to help us handle the problem. One month it was so bad-the exterminator caught 7 full-grown rats. They had built a nest somewhere in the attic. It was awful.

A few moments passed and the scratching stopped. I didn't think about it again. I got up, went to the kitchen, then went to my bedroom to get dressed and back to the kitchen again. I did that a lot. I would go over and over to see if there was anything different in the refrigerator. Of course, there was nothing, but still; I always did it as if something to eat would magically appear. As I walked out the door, I heard the scratching sound, again and again. But like before, I didn't think anything of it. I stepped out of my place, locked it, and was on my way.

2

It was a beautiful day. The sun was violently bright and the sky was a warm blue as if it had swallowed the ocean and held it within itself throughout the day. Alex didn't live too far away, so I walked to his house.

I knocked on Alex's door and he immediately opened it.

"Good to see you," Alex greeted me as I walked inside his house.

"Same here."

"Are you hungry?" Alex asked. He always had food. He always had everything and to be honest, I think this was why it didn't matter that he wasn't going to school. Both of his parents were very successful and they had the biggest house on the block. It was as if they couldn't hide their wealth, like a neon sign the size of a pickup truck advertised, "we are rich" in bold letters. Besides, everyone knew Alex's parents were loaded and the several luxury cars parked on their porch kind of gave it away.

"Well, what do you want to do?" Alex asked.

"I'm not sure. Do you want to head out back and play some basketball?"

"Sure, there's nothing else to do, unless you want to just hang out and drink my father's liquor? You know I'm always up for that."

Alex and I had a drinking problem. Well . . . it wasn't so much a problem. It was more like a hobby. Whenever we were together, we would take a few shots of his father's liquor. We did this almost every time we had the chance.

BEAUTIFUL AND DAMNED

Our faces went numb and everything was how it should be. Alex being four shots in and I being five, we found ourselves sitting on the couch listening to music.

"Do you ever get bored of life?" Alex asked.

"What do you mean?" I replied and laughed because I thought his question was ridiculous.

"Like, do you ever feel like all of this, I mean, what we are doing with our time, should be more? I mean do you ever feel bored with everything and everyone? Or is it just me?"

"I think you've lost your mind, either that, or you're too drunk, you've gone off the deep end, and I can't pull you out of this one," I said, laughing more. Of course, I was kidding around, but still, it was funny to me because Alex was beginning to sound like a philosopher and he had failed philosophy when he was in school a few months back.

"Where is all of this coming from?" I said with a more serious note.

"I was talking to Eddie--"

"Oh god, Eddie? Are you serious?" I rolled my eyes. Eddie was a complete moron and I think I hated him, no wait, I *know* I hated him. I would avoid him at all cost. Everything about him annoyed me. You know when you meet someone for the first time and you just don't like them; you can't find anything interesting about them? Well, that was Eddie to me. Everything, and by that I mean *everything,* about him was disturbing. It drove me mad.

"You still talk to that guy?" I quickly asked.

"Yeah, he comes by every once in a while," Alex murmured as his gaze fell to the ground.

"To be honest, I don't even want to know what he told you. I mean the kid is a shit-head. I don't even know why you hang out with him."

"No one likes him, that I know, but for some reason, I feel sorry for him. I mean, there was a time when I wanted to kill the guy, but then, I kind of started feeling bad for him. So I became his friend. Well, I tried to be his friend and then he kind of just grew on me like some kind of weed that bloomed into a rose. Or maybe I'm just used to him and I'm blind to the fact that he is an idiot. I don't know; I can't call it," said Alex.

"Just don't bring him around me, please." I took my phone out of my pocket to check my social media.

"Hey, it's getting late. I should get going," I said.

BEAUTIFUL AND DAMNED

"It's only 10. You're leaving already?"

"Yeah, I have to go. I have some things to do at home," I lied. I had nothing to do at home. I just felt like leaving. There was only so much time I could give and that time was up. I was like that. I would go out and then just want to leave. Sometimes I wanted to talk and then, out of nowhere, I wanted to be left alone. I was like that with almost everything. I was a walking contradiction. But almost everyone was like that. No one ever knew what they wanted and when they received whatever it was they were anticipating, they wanted more or less.

"Okay, I'm heading out. We'll talk tomorrow; maybe we'll go to the mall or something." I got up from the couch and headed straight for the door.

"Yeah, just call me or come straight here, I'll be getting up by 8."

"Okay, sounds good. Talk soon." I replied as I walked out of the house and Alex closed the door.

The walk home wasn't too bad. I was pissed drunk and hurt my foot by walking right into a fire hydrant. Soon enough, I remembered that I hadn't called my parents all day. It had flown over my head. I wasn't going to call them now, although they would always say to call them at anytime. But as usual I wasn't going to call them, especially while I was drunk out of my mind.

I made it home; I wasn't sure how, but I did. I wasn't feeling all that bad when I was sitting on Alex's couch, but by the time I got up to leave, the alcohol hit me, like a thousand 25-pound weights piling over me at once. This unwelcomed drowsiness crawled upon me and walked me home. I threw up twice on the way and it wasn't like it was a long walk, no, it wasn't, but it felt long enough.

By the time I was ready to go to sleep, I heard that strange sound coming from the wall and then I remembered how I had heard that same scratching sound right before I had left for Alex's. I didn't pay much attention to it. I was too drunk and too tired to give it any thought. So I closed my eyes and forgot it was there. I forgot the world was there and suddenly, I left my consciousness to the hands of the unknown. I was asleep and that was the end of it all.

3

"Wake up." A voice entered the room. It was a dark and deep voice, untruthful and bloodcurdling. I was lying on my bed dead asleep, beneath my covers and wrapped in between pillows. I did that often.

"Wake up, Joshua." I heard the voice again.

The television flickered with an ominous glow.

BEAUTIFUL AND DAMNED

"Who's there?"

"Hello Joshua, I'm Jacob." The voice was bold,
strong but light. I couldn't understand where it was
coming from. It was as if someone was standing right
behind me, speaking directly into my ear. I looked
behind me, but it was impossible for someone to be
standing there. My bed was pushed against the wall and
for a second, I thought how maybe I had left the window
open and one of my friends was playing a joke on me.

"There's no one out there," said the mysterious
voice.

I scanned the room. But it was difficult to see with
the eerie glow from the TV as my only light. I sat in
bed with my legs crossed.

"Who are you?" I said. I wasn't afraid but I *was*
shaken up a little. No one wants to wake up to
something like this and I wasn't one to scare easily,
but this was something else-I mean, I was alone in the
house, and now there was a dual-layered voice coming
from every direction.

"Don't be afraid, Joshua. I'm not here to harm you."

I tried to stay calm and figure out what was going
on. I couldn't tell if I was dreaming or if this was
really happening. I mean, it felt real, but there were

nights when I would dream so vividly that it, too, felt real.

"Who are you? And why are you here? Is this a dream?" My voice echoed through the dimmed room. I wanted to wake up but I couldn't, perhaps this was a dream within a dream and I hated those.

"I'm Jacob, the angel." The voice said. And then, I looked into my closet. The door was slightly cracked, just enough for me to see all the way through the back of the wall. I saw this being, a humanoid type figure and it was gently glowing, a somewhat neon color but it was very faint. It was as if it wasn't really there, transparent but still visible enough to notice it, that is, if you were paying attention. It was sitting on the floor by the corner in the closet and it wasn't facing me, it was facing the wall. It had no hair and no clothes on. It did have ears, arms, feet, fingers and toes.

"If you're an angel, then where are your wings?" I didn't know what to say. I said the most obvious thing that came to my mind. By now, I was a bit frightened, but still, it wasn't enough to shake me off completely. Perhaps, all of this was just an unusual dream, I thought, and because of it, I went along with the stream.

"This is not a dream," said Jacob as he stood up, still facing the wall. He must have been at least 7 feet tall, medium built, and his head nearly touched the ceiling of my closet.

"Why can't I see your face? Why can't you turn around and come out of the closet," I said to Jacob.

"I can't," said Jacob. He stood there not moving.

"You can't? Why not? Why can't you?"

"I have no face."

"Everyone has a face," I muttered.

"I don't. I'm not everyone," said Jacob. As he spoke, a horrifying chill raced down my spine.

"Why are you here Jacob? Is this real? Are you real?" I had to ask again.

"Yes, I'm real. I've been here since the beginning of everything and since the beginning of you. I've seen the past. I've seen the future. I'm all that defines you and you are all that defines me. We are connected." His voice was haunting and a settling darkness arose from his words. It was a terrible feeling, one I wouldn't have bestowed upon my worst enemy.

"What do you want with me?"

"I just need someone to talk to. I feel empty sometimes, broken and alone."

"Okay, we can talk," I replied. I thought that perhaps if I spoke to this aberration that maybe it would enlighten me a little. Although frightened, I was a bit curious about what this thing wanted and after all, I was a bit curious to what was going on.

"How did you get in here, Jacob?" I asked.

"I can go anywhere. All I have to do is think of a place and I'm there, but only if I have to . . . only if I must," said Jacob.

I wasn't sure what to make of it. All I could think about was turning on the lights and walking straight into the closet. I wanted to pull Jacob out, but my intuition told me not to go in there.

"What do you mean you can go anywhere?"

"If I explained it, you wouldn't be able to understand it. If I showed you, you still wouldn't believe it. So the question is, what do you want to believe? What do you want to see?"

"What do you know?" I asked in the most esteemed voice.

"What if I told you the world was going to end in two days, Joshua?" said Jacob.

"How is that?"

"It will end soon enough and it will end between a whisper and a loud bang."

"You're right; I don't understand."

"I don't expect you to. No one *ever* does."

"So what do you mean the world will end?" It wasn't everyday where you heard someone saying the world was going to end. Dream or not, it was just something I wanted to know.

"I'll tell you in two days. Until then, I'll be watching you," said Jacob and he slowly walked through the wall and in an instant was gone. I couldn't believe what I had just seen. Did I just experience something supernatural? Or was it all just a dream? I didn't know what to think.

I was wide awake. I couldn't sleep. I got up and did a few things to keep my mind busy and it worked. Within an hour, I was fast asleep and I didn't think about Jacob for the rest of the night.

4

The following day, I did the usual. I got up a little later than I expected. I went to the kitchen, made myself something to eat, and stayed in my living room for about three hours. Within that time, I thought about my parents--how I still hadn't called them. But what I found even stranger they hadn't called me since they left. Maybe they forgot about me? Or maybe they were too busy. I thought about Jacob and what he said. "The world will end in two days." And every time I thought about this, I had this disturbing flashback-- Jacob didn't have a face. His disturbing voice was buried in my thoughts and every time I forgot about him, the thought of him burrowed in deeper. I couldn't get it out of my head. Why me? Why would this supernatural experience happen to me? I mean, all my life I have lived an ordinary life and I have been an ordinary person. I didn't understand this.

Early afternoon, I decided to go to Alex's house. I didn't call. I just got dressed and walked on over.

I knocked on Alex's door. I waited outside. What was taking him so long? I knew he was home; he was *always* home. I knocked again and I waited. Then, I heard a stomping sound coming from within. The door cracked.

"Come inside," said Alex. His voice was relaxed and his eyelids slightly closed because of the sun.

BEAUTIFUL AND DAMNED

We sat down on his couch, with nothing much to do, but I did, in fact, have much to say.

"I had this strange experience last night. Or maybe it was a dream. It was so vivid that I thought it was real," I said.

"What do you mean?"

"Something happened last night and it spooked me. I know this is going to sound a little crazy, but I think I was visited by an extraterrestrial or some sort of ghost. All I know is, if it was a dream, then it felt real, or maybe it was the liquor. I did come home really drunk last night," I said. "It told me the world was going to end in two days. How crazy is that?"

Alex stared into my eyes as if his soul was communicating with mine. "The world is not going to end," his voice was strong and bold.

Alex was obviously confident the world wasn't going to end and maybe it wasn't, but who was he to say it wasn't? Maybe it was. Everyday there is a fifty percent chance for everything. You either live or die, fall or rise, love or hate, and you either live in a dream world or a real one. And who is to say this reality, our reality, isn't a dream? Or vice versa? No one can answer that. Everything is 50/50 and the probabilities are endless. "We wouldn't really know that would we?" I stood behind my 50/50 theory as if my life depended on it.

"Do you know how many times religious cults and the media have predicted the world was going to end? Remember the year 2000? Remember 2012? Remember 2015 with CERN and the god particle? Wasn't that supposed to end the world? Right? But it didn't, right? C'mon-an eerie dream shouldn't shake you like this," said Alex. For a guy that wasn't in school, he made a lot of sense.

"I think you're right, but it still frightens me a little." I looked out the window. My eyes were drawn to the movement of the trees.

"If you want, I'll stay over with you tonight," said Alex as he shook his hand in front of my face to get my attention. "Hey!"

"Yeah, that sounds good."

"Okay, great. Then you'll see how it was all just a dream and it's really nothing to be worried about."

The rest of the day we stayed in. We had a few drinks and talked so much that we barely had time for anything else. Alex and I dove into a conversation about life. It was brief, but it was still something to think about.

"Do you ever think of death?" I said. I didn't know where this question came from. It was an accidental question, but it just spluttered out of me, as if it was a question that had to be asked.

"I think about it but not too much. Why? Josh, are you okay? I mean, first, you tell me about aliens visiting you at night, then how much you hate school, and then how careless your parents are. Should I be concerned?" Alex asked as he smirked and laughed.

"Yeah, you're right. I've been intense all day. It must have been the drinking from last night that got me into this funk," I said.

There were times when I would drink and then the next day feel as if I wasn't myself--as if I was out of my body and I'd watch myself slowly drift away with the clouds. But there were also times, even without the liquor, when I felt this way too, and those were the times where I needed someone the most. Those were the times I didn't go to school, the times I would lock myself within myself and see if someone would care enough to save me.

5

Alex gathered his things and shoved them into a bag. He grabbed a bottle of whiskey, his toothbrush, toothpaste, and a few water bottles.

"We're going to need these," he said as he opened the refrigerator and grabbed a bucket filled with chicken wings. I thought it was weird because Alex knew how much I didn't like chicken wings. Either way, I continued to wait for him to finish.

"Ready?" I said as I waited by the door. My left foot tapped the floor. I was anxious to get home. I needed to call my parents. I hadn't heard from them in two days.

"Yeah, now I'm ready. Let's get going."

"Okay," I replied as Alex locked his door.

By the time we settled in it was already 10 p. m. and the first thing I did was look at my answering machine for any missed calls or any voice messages, but to my surprise, there were none.

"No one called?" Alex said.

"No. Weird."

"Why don't you call your parents?" Alex asked, and I just shrugged.

"Well, that's okay. So where do you want me to sleep, in your room? On the floor?"

"I'm not sure. We'll figure it out when we get tired."

"Okay and you'll see how everything was all in your head."

"Right!" I said, sarcastic enough.

Alex made himself at home. He took out the whiskey bottle, placed his bag on my mother's couch, and walked into my kitchen. He grabbed a cup, filled it with ice, and poured some of the whiskey.

"You want a drink?"

"No, I've had enough. Did I not tell you about last night?" I said with sarcasm.

"Yeah, okay," said Alex, rolling his eyes. He always did that and I hated it. I could tell this was going to be a long night. Not because I was already annoyed with Alex and his drinking, but because my parents hadn't called me. I was worried about them. I even thought about giving them a ring. I grabbed my cell phone and began to dial my mother's number. It rang four times and I was forwarded to voicemail.

"My parents didn't pick up the phone. It forwarded to voicemail. Don't you think that's strange?" I said. I felt bewildered.

"That's strange. I wonder why they would have done that. I'm sure they're okay and they know you're okay as well. If not, they wouldn't have left you alone. Believe me," said Alex.

"Yeah, okay. I'm not going to freak out. I just think it's not normal, but yeah, you have a point. I'm just not going to think about it. I mean, what could go wrong? By the time I know it, they're back, and I'm going to be wishing they weren't here. So let me enjoy this moment and forget all of that and you know what? I think I'll take you up on that drink," I said as I grabbed a cup and filled it with ice.

Alex poured me a drink and we didn't stop drinking until the light in our eyes faded and the world became nothing more than a figment of our reality.

6

"Wake up, Joshua."

I opened my eyes to see Jacob sitting on the edge of the couch. Again, he faced the wall. I slowly stood up. Alex was sound asleep on the floor. We were in my living room. It was dark and the only visible light was the one coming from the street lamp outside of the main window. The curtains fluttered, caught in the blowing air from the air conditioner. Jacob appeared and disappeared as the curtains moved. The light slightly

shined upon him. He didn't say a word for a few moments
and those moments felt like a lifetime.

"Tomorrow, the world will end, Joshua," his voice
was husky and guttural. Although I had already seen
Jacob, there was something disturbing about his energy.
Something about him and his presence was ominous,
disembodied, and daunting. I took a look closer as he
sat on the end of the couch as if he were leaping on
the edge of a skyscraper. His arms were folded and his
head faced down. He didn't move. He looked heavy but
weightless, and again, he looked as if he wasn't here,
but he was.

"I'm going to wake up my friend," I said.

Jacob sat there and did nothing, said nothing.

"Why are you here? I don't understand. Is this real?
Is this really happening right now?" I couldn't grasp
any of it. It was a faint nightmare. I couldn't connect
the dots. I couldn't tell where this was going and
above all, I wasn't sure if I wanted it to stop. My
life was lived in such a way that I had no excitement,
no real cause or real story to be exact. All my life, I
had been living like a ghost, one with no place to go
and no place to build a life in. I felt as if I had no
true purpose and what was worse was how I actually was
starting to believe Jacob. Deep down inside, I believed
his end of the world prediction. I just didn't want to
be too naive and fall into that blindly.

"Don't worry about Alex; I will be seeing him soon," said Jacob.

"So why don't you tell me why you're really here?" I pulled my knees up to my chest and wrapped my arms around them.

"I don't want you to be afraid, Joshua."

"I'm trying not to be," I said, but of course, it was easier said than done. As if being woken up by a strange presence wasn't terrifying enough. I had heard of supernatural experiences and I had never experienced one, not until now. I now understood that sometimes people who talked about such experiences aren't crazy. How maybe the rest of the world *is* crazy. I mean, that is, if you can see such things other people aren't capable of seeing, then maybe that must count for something.

"Let me tell you a story." Jacob insisted. "In 1854 there was a couple. They had been together for over 60 years. I saw them since they were born, as all who are born. I watched them grow and I watched them become more and that was the first time I ever did that, the first time in a long time, to be exact..."

"Done what?"

"Manifest." Jacob dragged this word in a slow hiss.

"Manifest?"

"Yes, Joshua. I am manifesting to you, as well."

"I don't understand," I said, but lately
understanding anything had been a concept that I hadn't
been able to grasp, for everything I had been going
through just made things worse, made things more
confusing for me.

"So what happened to this couple? And what do they
have to do with me?" I asked, interested.

"I will tell you the rest tomorrow."

"Why tomorrow? Why not now?" I demanded.

"I will tell you the rest before it begins, before
the end of it all shores," Jacob said firmly. He slowly
stood up and vanished into the creases of my living
room wall. By the time Jacob was gone, I was wide
awake. I wanted to wake up Alex, but he was sound
asleep, so I simply stared at him. *Why hadn't I
awakened him when Jacob was here*? I wanted to tell Alex
what had just happened but knew he'd tell me it was all
a dream. But it wasn't a dream. Jacob was real, I was
real, and Alex was real. And we were all just trying to
make sense of this place, trying to understand why such
things do happen.

7

The sun beamed through the window and the loud rumble coming from the air conditioner woke me. Alex was still asleep on the floor. I glanced at the clock; it was almost noon. I got up to use the restroom and then went back to the couch.

"Alex." I whispered. "Alex, wake up." I shoved him.

"Yeah, yeah, I'm up," he said. He was half awake as he grunted his words.

"Alex, wake up I have to tell you something," I said as he kicked his legs and flipped on his other side.

"It's important."

"What could be important at this time of the day?" He said as he shoved his head beneath the pillows.

"I saw the entity last night. The one I told you about, remember?"

"Huh? It's a little too early for that, don't you think?"

"It's noon. C'mon, wake up."

"All right," he mumbled. He stood up stretching both arms toward the ceiling. He yawned twice, cracked his back, and snapped his neck side to side. The sounds were gruesome. My face shriveled into itself as he continued to stretch.

"Okay, now I'm up. What were you saying?" he said.

"That thing came back to me last night and it told me the world was going to end today."

"You're still on that? The world isn't going to end. I told you already; that's not how it works. No one can decide that. C'mon, now!"

I felt foolish saying these things to Alex, but it was the truth. There was no other way to explain it. I just needed someone to listen to me. Even if it wasn't real, which I was sure it was, I just needed someone to talk to. Someone not to tell me what it was I saw or felt or whatever I was going through. I just needed someone, anyone, to tell me how everything was going to be okay.

"It sat on the edge of the couch and told this story and then he just stopped. He said he'd finish the story before it begins."

"Before it begins? What on earth are you talking about? What does that even mean?"

"I think he meant before the world ends," I said.

Alex gave me this look, this indirect look as if he was suggesting I was crazy. "I think you need to clear your mind. Why don't we go to the boardwalk? Maybe we can get something to eat, walk around, you know? Like the old times, before things were complicated."

"Yeah, I'd like that. Let's go."

"Okay, but first I have to go home. I'll pick you up in one of my father's cars. Okay?"

"Yeah, sounds good, okay!"

The rest of the day went well. We *did* go to the boardwalk. We ate and walked around. We *did* feel as we once did when things were less complicated. There was something about the boardwalk and the ocean. The way the waves crashed upon the shore, the way the smaller children would laugh and play, and the way the air felt as it passed through our fingers and hair. It brought back memories, the good kind, the ones I couldn't distance myself from even if I wanted to. And that's why I loved this part of my city so much because there are some things you can't heal on your own and then there's the ocean. If you listened close enough, sometimes the waves revealed all the answers you have been looking for, all you had to do was listen with your heart and not your ears.

Maybe I loved this place so much because when I was younger my mother and father would bring me here and now being here after so long, I felt a little sentimental and nostalgic. Maybe I was supposed to be here today with Alex and maybe everything I'd been experiencing for the last few days was not as intense as I thought them to be. In fact, this wasn't the first time I had seen something completely out of mind. Every so often, I felt as if I was being watched and there were times when I would encounter strange things. Although this was slightly different, I definitely wasn't a stranger to odd things.

By the time we decided to leave, the sun had gone down, and the boardwalks lights lit the sky. The people walking the boardwalk gave me a sense of being alive. I didn't want to go. It was one of those nights, the ones that would haunt you forever. It was that beautiful. It was like poetry and I was reminded how important it was to live in the moment. After all, our lives were defined by an accumulation of moments, both bad and good. And tonight was a good one and because of this night, I appreciated Alex more. He pulled me out of this net. He truly was a good friend and it was moments like these when a friend became more than just a good friend. It was moments like these when a friend became a savior, when a friend became family.

During the drive home, all that had made me blue had dissipated. I didn't think about Jacob. I didn't reflect on why my parents hadn't contacted me. I didn't think about missing school or anything like that. All I thought about was getting home and looking forward to a night where I was finally able to find peace.

8

I was at Alex's house. He was going to give me this old Wu-Tang CD. It was called *Enter the 36 Chambers*. We stayed outside for a little bit and talked. I was calmer. I found myself in a place where I once was before. Maybe tonight Alex saved me. Maybe tonight the world wasn't going to end but begin. All days offered second chances and maybe a friend is the only person who can remind you how every day is a new day and how every day there's is a new path, a new way to find yourself.

"Well, I have to get going. It's getting late and I'm tired. The beach and the sun wore me out today," I said.

"Yeah, okay. Call me tomorrow as soon as you wake up. Or anytime during the night if you need someone to talk to," said Alex.

"You know, you're a really good friend. And I know there are times when we don't see eye to eye, but I just want you to know, you're a good person, and you deserve the world," I said as Alex laughed.

"What I deserve is my father's car, but thanks, and that's what friends are for. I got your back, always, no matter what."

"Thank you for everything and thank you for your friendship. I have always admired you for your kindness." I gave Alex a hug, showing him how much I valued his friendship and in an instant, I passed through his front door and walked away.

9

The moon was full and a black haze muted it. The trees bent in the breeze and a dead silence filled the street. The street lamps were dimmed and the sidewalks were covered in leaves. I brushed them aside as I walked through. I was the only thing giving the street life and movement. I felt as if everything watched me: the buildings, the concrete, the trees, and the bushes. They observed every step, every breath, and every thought. Even the moon, wearing its hazy jacket, appeared to be stalking me.

When I got home, I stood outside the door and thought about Jacob. I thought about what he had told me: about the end of the world and how the night was almost over. I reached down into my pockets to get a hold of my keys, when suddenly I heard his voice.

"Hello, Joshua." It was as if Jacob was right behind me. I could almost feel his breath. I stood still, which was the only thing my instinct told me to do.

"Do you remember the story I was telling you?" Jacob asked.

"Yes, yes I do, but you told me you would finish it right before the world ends. You stopped when you said you had manifested," I said, not moving. I was petrified. My body became like stone and my legs anchored themselves into the ground. I didn't look back. I didn't have enough courage to do so.

"Let me continue from where I left off." He was silent for a moment. "It was the first time I had manifested in decades. I was going against the rules. I'm not supposed to manifest and the only reason I did was because I saw myself in them. From the moment I manifested, I befriended the two, and I came to the conclusion that we are all the same, no matter what we are. We all tend to feel empty from time to time. And because of that, I felt pain for the couple," Jacob said.

"I don't understand where all of this is going and what the end of the world has to do with this."

"It has everything to do with this and by me manifesting, I feel as if I, too, am alive, as if I, too, am near the end."

"What are you, Jacob?" I asked as I slowly placed my hands into my pocket. Facing my door and listening to Jacob from behind-my fear had fallen to the ground. I became moved by what he was saying.

"It's not what I am. It's more like who I am."

"Then who are you, Jacob?" The street lamps began to flicker and a deadly whisper filled the air as I inhaled.

"Joshua, I'm the angel of death and I am here to take you, as I took that couple," Jacob whispered. Suddenly a bolt of lightning ran through my body. The first thing I did was run--I ran from my house, through the same empty streets, through Alex's house and I kept running and running and I didn't look back. I was terrified. My throat swelled and sweat flooded my face and body.

By the time I came to a complete stop, I was on the golf course. I wasn't thinking as I ran, I just wanted to get as far as possible and that I did, but it didn't help, because when I stopped to cool down, Jacob was already there, waiting.

"Don't kill me. I'm too young to die," I pleaded for my life in hopes that Jacob would grant me some mercy. "Please don't kill me!" I yelled. I fell to my knees as Jacob began to walk toward me.

"I'm not here to kill you, Joshua. I'm here to take you. Do you remember when I said the world was going to end?" Jacob said as he took his final steps toward me. Tears began to flood my eyes. I couldn't fathom what was going on. Everything moved too fast and my mind flashed. Fragments of my life appeared then dissolved like dimming photographs.

"Yes, I remember," I said as I inhaled and exhaled rapidly.

"Your world will end in a whisper and a loud bang Joshua," said Jacob as he lifted his left hand. Right before his fingers touched my forehead; I looked into the faceless figure and saw a million faces, all welcoming me into the light. It felt like home, like a welcoming party, and everyone I had ever met was waiting for me on the other side. And then, without a moment to realize what was actually happening, I said hello in a whisper, and a loud bang clouded the golf course and just like that, the world became dark, and I was gone.

10

It had been a few months since Joshua's death and since then, Alex took it upon himself and believed it was entirely his fault. He beat himself over the head day in and day out and each night and every night after, as well. Alex had become a different person. He visited Joshua's parents on a weekly basis and he never forgave himself, although many people would tell him there was nothing he could have done, that it was all meant to happen.

"Alex, so what happened to Josh? I heard about it and I'm sorry for your loss but how did he die?" asked Valerie, a sophomore from Gemballa High.

"Yeah, what happened to him?" asked Matt, another student who went to Joshua's high school.

Alex didn't want to talk about it, but he did take the time to answer them.

"He was found dead in the golf course by my house. He shot himself with his father's pistol," Alex said with a flat voice.

"Wow, that's sad to hear, my condolences."

"Yeah, I mean, I wish I would have known he was going through something. That week he wasn't acting like himself. He was saying a lot of strange things and out of nowhere, he spoke to me about death. I didn't pay much attention. God, I wish I had. Sometimes I feel like I could have saved him. I mean, I *know* I could have saved him. I was his best friend and only a best friend can save a friend from total destruction. I *know* I could have, I just *know* it!" Tears streamed from Alex's eyes. It was hard for him to talk about Joshua.

By the time Alex arrived home. He did what he usually did. He called Joshua's mother to wish her a good night and spoke to her for a while. It was always hard to hang up the phone knowing the depth of pain Joshua's parents were undergoing. Soon enough, Alex hung up and went directly to his couch. This was also something he did every night. He stayed there and watched television until he felt drowsy and then he would walk to his bed and fall asleep. But tonight was different. Tonight, Alex had fallen asleep on his couch. It took about three hours for Alex to wake up and when he did, he went into his kitchen because he hadn't eaten all day. His hunger pang was violent and perhaps that was what woke him up to being with. As he entered the kitchen, he heard a light scratching sound coming from the center of the wall, but, Alex being Alex, he paid no attention to this and opened the refrigerator.

Another scratching sound--but Alex still paid no attention and continued to go through his refrigerator. For a third time, a scratching came from the wall behind him and this time it was loud enough to catch his attention. He turned to see what it was. It was then, that he heard a voice coming from the other end of his kitchen.

"Hello Alex, I'm Jacob." The voice was bold, strong but light, haunting and hard to forget. Alex stood there, frozen and terrified. Jacob slowly came from inside the wall. He stopped a few inches from Alex and then, close enough, Jacob, being over 7 feet tall, leaned over Alex and whispered. "What if I told you the world was going to end in two days, Alex?" Jacob said.

Alex stood there in shock and didn't say a word.

LOST AND FOUND

1

Already late for her job's Christmas Eve party, Jennifer searched for late minute items. She glanced in the mirror. Looking perfect was a must. The executives attended these parties and she wanted to make a first-rate impression. After all, this would be the first time she would meet them.

She wore a breathtaking velvet dress with a slit that ran up to her mid-thigh. The open back added an element of sexiness and her hair was swept into the sweetest French twist. Her sparkly shoes matched the deep purple of her dress and her lips looked stained with wine. With its natural glow, her skin was soft as cashmere and her eyes a honey-gold. She took one last peek in the mirror and was finally satisfied. She looked like a pleasant dream.

Sharing the couch with Mattel, her 15-year-old Labrador retriever, she clicked on the TV. He had his usual half the couch. His spot. Where he spent most of his days.

"That lazy dog had his life handed to him. He doesn't know how good he has it."

Jennifer would tell her friends when they visited, "He's been pampered his entire life. He eats only raw and organic food, drinks bottled water, and I walk him around the block twice a day."

He's lived better than me, better than most people I know, she thought with a smile. After all, he deserved to be spoiled.

She scratched Mattel on his head and he, being the lethargic dog that he was, crawled towards her lap without using his back legs. Once situated, Mattel turned on his back for Jennifer to rub him. As Jennifer pet him, she noticed that, once again, he hadn't touched his food. He had been like this most of the week. This was relatively unusual, but when it had happened in the past, she would take him to the vet.

"It's okay if your dog doesn't eat for a few days," the vet had said. "He's an old dog. It's completely normal that his appetite has slowed. Just be sure you change his food and water daily."

Which Jennifer did--at least twice a day. The more she thought about what the doctor had said, the less his disinterest in food bothered her. So, instead of heading for the vet like she usually did, she didn't pay too much attention to it.

A half hour passed and it was time to head to the party. She took one last look in the mirror, grabbed her purse, and turned to Mattel.

"Mattel, now be a good boy. Mommy will be back soon."

It was a ritual that she and Mattel shared. Every time she left the house, she reminded him to be good. As if Mattel understood, Jennifer always came home to a calm house.

2

She arrived at the lobby of the Hyatt, Miami Beach, a bit before 6 p. m. and the first thing that caught her attention was the lights. It was as if she entered a magical world. The entire lobby twinkled like fireflies dancing beneath the night sky, like stars on a moonless night, like fairies with small lanterns. Everything glowed. Tonight would be a night to remember.

The bar was elegant, a dark burgundy with a craftsmanship that looked as if it were built in the medieval ages. People packed around it as they waited in line for their drinks.

Pushing through the crowd, she finally made it to the bar line. *I think I'll have a Cabernet*, she thought.

A co-worker walked in and immediately hurried toward her.

"Jenn! You look stunning!" Said Michael, the department's lead software developer. He was well groomed with his hair slicked to the back.

"Thanks Mike. Hey, have you seen anyone else from work?" Her voice was low and shy.

"No, I just got in, but it looks like it's going to be a full house. It's sensational, isn't it?" He said.

"Yes, it is. I love what they have done with the lights."

"Yeah, let's take a picture. You and the lights."

"Now?"

"Yeah, now, c'mon." Michael grabbed her as he took his phone out from his back pocket.

"Say cheese!" he yelled as the flash nearly blinded her.

She didn't want him to take a photo, but it happened so quickly, she had no choice.

"Well, I'll see you later," she said to Michael as the line brought her closer to the bar. "If you got the lights, send me a copy of that picture."

"Yeah, sure thing. Have fun and Merry Christmas, Jenn."

He walked into the crowd and disappeared like a distant memory as he faded into the waves of people.

She sensed that it was going to be a great night, but perhaps awkward since she didn't recognize anyone. But she always looked on the bright side of things and knew her co-workers would soon arrive.

3

For a company event, it was quite the bash. After having done her obligatory chats with the executives, she sat at a table with her co-workers and finally relaxed. It was about midnight and the party was still going. By now, Jennifer had had one too many drinks and the room seemed to spin slowly.

"Jenny, are you okay?" asked Maria, her half-drunk supervisor.

BEAUTIFUL AND DAMNED

"I don't know. I don't feel too well. Maybe I should go home . . . or do you think I should wait it out?"

Her face was pale. She was sweating.

"Yeah, you don't look too good. I'll get you some water," said Claudia, a bespectacled intern in a mini-dress. She headed toward the bar.

Claudia returned with the water and some cheese snacks.

"Here drink this and eat something," said Claudia, not wanting to draw attention to Jennifer.

Without making a scene, Claudia opened the water and handed it to Jennifer. No one, besides her friends, had noticed how much Jennifer actually had to drink.

She downed the water as if she'd spent the last hour dragging herself across a desert.

"You know, I usually don't get this drunk. I know how to control myself. It's just that I haven't eaten anything and I've been trying to lose weight." Jennifer finished the bottle of water and placed it on top of the table. Her eyes drooped and her words slurred slightly, but ultimately, she felt like she could sober up before it was time to leave.

"It's okay, it happens to the best of us," slurred Maria.

After 45 minutes had passed, Jennifer felt better. Three water bottles in, a lot of restroom visits, and she was as good as new.

"I should get going," said Jennifer.

"Yeah, me too, the party's just about dead, anyway," Maria added.

Parties were like that, one moment they started and the next, they ended--the same way all things ended-- slowly, yet fast, and then, just like that, between the seconds that brought them to us, they're gone. They go away and all we can do is remember how they once made us feel.

Jennifer grabbed her things.

"You sure you're okay?" asked Maria one last time.

"Yeah, I'm fine. Trust me, I've been worse, a lot worse."

"Okay, text me when you get home," Maria said firmly.

"Okay, I will."

Jennifer went around the room wishing everyone a Merry Christmas and a Happy New Year.

She walked out of the Hyatt, looked back at the lights, and smiled. It was such a gorgeous night and although she'd never get this moment back, she knew she'd remember it. She saw herself in the lights-for their shimmer in the bleak winter and their promise of hope. She said goodbye as she got further from the party and closer to her car. As she turned out of the Hyatt's parking lot, she peered into the rearview mirror and the lights still spoke to her. She felt good and was happy for that very moment--a moment she knew she would hang on to forever.

4

By the time she arrived home, it was well past 2 a.m. She unlocked her door, headed straight for the shower, and brushed her teeth. She washed her face, again. This time, to remove the residue her makeup left behind.

She put on her pajamas and right before she jumped into bed to call it a night, she realized that Mattel hadn't greeted her at the door. "Mattel, c'mon boy! Where are you?"

She heard nothing.

"Mattel? C'mon, boy . . . c'mon . . ." Not certain where Mattel was, she walked through her apartment.

"Mattel?" She looked on to the balcony. He sometimes fell asleep there. But he wasn't on the balcony, under the bed, or behind the sofa. *"Where could he have gone to?"* she thought as she walked all over her apartment.

She felt a hollow sensation in the pit of her belly. It felt like a dagger plunged into the center of her soul. The first thing that crossed her mind: perhaps her parents had passed by and accidentally left the door opened and Mattel had escaped. (It wasn't the first time he had escaped. He had done so several times when he was younger.)

She grabbed the phone to call her father and just before the first ring, she noticed Mattel lying on the floor in her closet.

She quickly hung up and ran to him.

"Mattel what's wrong?" She gently rubbed his ears and listened to his breathing. He panted vigorously.

Worried, she mustered whatever energy she had left and lifted him from the ground. She was going to take him to the 24-hour animal hospital, a few blocks away.

She managed to get him in the car and drove quickly to the hospital. Although filled with anxiety, she tried to stay calm.

He probably ate some socks, she thought. *And now, he just has a stomachache. Either way, I'm going to take him in just to be sure that he's okay.*

She tried to convince herself that this was nothing. *It would soon be over*, she thought, and then they could both rest until morning.

5

The animal hospital was empty. Mattel was still panting, but she managed to get him to walk, at least far enough to get him through the vet's door.

"Jenny, how are you?" The receptionist asked as she leaned over and scratched Mattel's head.

Jenny shrugged.

"Hey Mattel, how are you good boy?

"So tell me, what's wrong with him?"

"I found him in the closet. He was panting like crazy. It freaked me out. Can you guys check him to make sure everything's okay? He hasn't been eating for the past few days. I mean, I know the doctor said that was expected, especially for his age, but can you have him check that out, too? Mattel's been acting weird."

"The doctor will check everything. Come on in and have a seat in this room here," said the receptionist as she opened the main door and directed Jenny into a private room.

She waited there patiently. Animal hospitals were the same as people hospitals--they took too long and when they finally saw you, it took but a few minutes and then, you are well on your way.

After thirty minutes, the vet finally came in. Jennifer explained what had happened and Mattel was taken in for procedural blood work.

Mattel was still in the back room when the doctor came back to the operatory to see Jennifer.

"There's something in his throat. We're going to get some x-rays. He could have eaten something and it hasn't fully gone down. We'll have answers shortly," said the vet as he flicked his pen and took a few notes.

Jennifer wasn't worried because she had the same thought. *Maybe he got into something he shouldn't have. All dogs were like that. Chewing things they shouldn't be chewing and getting into things they shouldn't be getting into. That's just how dogs were.*

About another 20 minutes passed and the doctor came into the operatory and closed the door. His expression had changed from happy-go-lucky to dry. The gray energy that followed him suggested bad news. Whenever a doctor closed the door, Jennifer had learned, it was never good news and she was sure, how this time, it wasn't good news.

"Jennifer, I'm sorry, but Mattel has a tumor in his throat and it's what is preventing him from eating."

"What? A tumor?" A streak of panic raced through her and disappeared into optimism. "Okay, what do we do? Surgery? You can remove it, right?" she said hopefully but deep down inside there was a sudden fracturing in her heart.

"We could, but considering his age there's only a 5% chance of survival and if he does survive, he would have to be fed through a syringe."

"What does that even mean? I don't understand."

"It's not recommended. The odds are against him."

"No--there must be *something* we can do!" Jennifer had begun to pace around the small room. "Chemo? People with cancer get treated with chemo. What about dogs?"

134

"It's too dangerous for a dog his age, Jennifer," the doctor murmured. "He's going to dehydrate and some other things can go wrong. My recommendation is to--"

"Put him to sleep?" said Jennifer, interrupting. Her voice was shrill.

"Yes. I'm sorry, but he's suffering. It's the most humane thing to do. We can do it now or you can have him pass at home. It's really up to you, okay? I'll have the tech come in and you can let him know your decision." The vet said, closing the door gently as he left the room.

Jennifer began to hyperventilate. She has had Mattel for 15 years. He was everything to her. She didn't want to put him down, but the thought of him suffering was horrid and to her, there was nothing worse than having him go through such pain. Her eyes sunk and she felt as if she had lost herself. Everything she had inside her-her hope, her optimism--was being ripped apart. Devastated, she had no choice but to put him down. He had run his course and had lived a pretty good life. About 5 minutes passed when Chad, the vet tech entered the room.

"I'm sorry to hear about Mattel." The tech said sympathetically. No one ever wants to hear this type of news.

"I've decided to put him down now, but I'd like to see him first," Jennifer said, trying to control her breath.

"Yes, of course."

"Will it hurt him?" Jennifer asked as a stream of endless tears fell from her eyes and she cried as if she had been holding in this kind of pain for several years.

"No, honey, it won't hurt him. It's fast and humane. He won't feel a thing. He'll pass peacefully." He placed his hand on Jennifer's shoulder, lightly comforting her.

"Can I be with him when you--? I want him to know that I'm there. I don't want him to go through it alone."

"Absolutely."

"Okay . . ."

"I'll bring him in, but first you have to sign these papers." The tech handed Jennifer a clipboard and pen.

"Okay . . ."

Jennifer signed all the papers and returned them to the tech.

"I'll come back with Mattel."

"Okay . . ."

Mattel was brought in with an IV attached to his front paw. The moment Jennifer saw him she began to sob. She hugged him and hugged him so tightly.

"You don't even know what's going on . . . you just don't know, baby . . . and that's what hurts the most. You're just here and you don't know how much you will be missed."

Her tears were continual. There was no end to her sadness. It burned a hole into her heart, one with such depth that no one, no matter who, *no one* would ever be able to fill it.

The doctor and the tech came in, ready to euthanize Mattel. Jennifer lifted Mattel and walked with him into another room in the back of the office. As they got there, the vet turned around and softly said...

"It's never easy for an owner to do this. Just know that what you're doing is the right thing," the vet said, his voice was filled with compassion.

"I know . . . I know . . ."

BEAUTIFUL AND DAMNED

The tech closed the door as he asked Jennifer to place Mattel on the table, which she did. He lay there, panting heavily, as the doctor prepared the procedure.

"This won't hurt him one bit."

Mattel's tail began to wag and his eyes locked with Jennifer's and only then had she noticed how Mattel had these different set of eyes, as if he had seen it all and as if he were able to look into her naked soul. She slowly whispered into his ear as more tears fell.

"Okay, Mattel, you've been a good boy and now it's time for you to go. Just remember, wherever it is we are meant to meet... just remember, to wait for me, and I promise to meet you there." Jennifer gave him a kiss on his forehead as the vet began to inject the preparation into the IV.

"This is painless. It will slow his heart," said the tech. Mattel's heart monitor kept beeping.

The vet slowly increased the dosage and Mattel's life began to fade away. Jennifer cried non-stop, it was as if a switch had been turned on, as if she couldn't control the stream that flowed out of her eyes. Mattel squealed a little in discomfort as the tech firmly held him down.

"It's okay, baby. Mama is still here with you." An overwhelming sadness surrounded her in a gloomy cloud.

Then, something happened and it was something
neither the vet nor the tech had ever seen. As the last
of the dose was pushed into the IV, Mattel, with all
his might, lifted his head and put his snout on
Jennifer's hand, as if he were thanking her for the
best life any dog had ever had... and then, in an
instant, he was gone. Jennifer was with him as he
welcomed the afterlife and she was left behind with
nothing more but a memory of what he once was.

6

A few weeks had passed. Jennifer had come to terms
with what had happened with Mattel. She knew she had
done the right thing. There would have been no way for
him to live a good life and Jennifer had no regrets. He
had given her his love and companionship and in the
end, although she could not save him, she kept him
alive in her heart.

As time went on--whenever she was alone--she
remembered Mattel, the lazy, old dog, the one she saved
and rescued as a puppy. But ultimately, she remembered
him as the kind and loving dog that he was. And because
of that, because of him, she was reminded how life was
too short and how every moment should be lived as if it
were her last. And in the end, she waited. She lived
her life waiting for that one moment where she and
Mattel would meet once again.

BEAUTIFUL AND DAMNED

And every time I look at you
I can feel something inside of me stirring.

I NEVER LEFT YOU

1

Like all things, it happened for a reason, and even the slightest mistake had a role in the grand scheme of things. All little stories were part of another short story that eventually would go back to an even bigger story. That's how this was.

Vanessa planned on staying home this Friday night. It had rained all day and through the night for the past several days. She didn't like going out in these terrible weather conditions. But when she watched the rain from her window, she always felt the temporary illusion of safety. She felt sheltered, nostalgic and at ease. Yes, she always loved the rain from inside but intensely disliked being out in it. In fact, she hadn't felt the rain in so long that she now feared its ability to soak through her, she feared that her stability would be shaken and that she'd be out of control.

Usually, especially after a hectic week at work, she would go to a bar on Friday nights to grab a drink with some friends. She was an Account Manager for Xerox corporate; a job she hated--but like most people, she had to do it regardless. It paid the bills.

Vanessa was home enjoying the rain. The storm was erratic; it would slowly fade out and when one thought it was over, it would return with thunderous force. It made her glad that she'd decided to stay home. The last thing she wanted was to be stuck in her car when the storm hit.

Vanessa sat on her cozy couch, deep into the cushions. She felt nothing could ruin such a tranquil evening, but then her phone rang, slicing through her peaceful night. *I should have left it on silent*, she thought.

It was Rachel and it kept getting louder with each ring.

Enjoying the sound of the rain hitting her balcony's awning, Vanessa reluctantly picked up the phone.

"Hello?"

"What are you doing tonight?" Rachel ignored Vanessa's greeting and went into her customary Rachel-wants-to-go-out conversation.

"Nothing. Have you seen the weather outside? It's raining bricks."

"Oh, c'mon. Your Friday night plan is to do *nothing*?"

"Yeah, I'm staying in tonight. Like I said, have you not checked outside? It looks like the end of the world."

Vanessa wasn't interested in going out, but she was curious to know what Rachel was up to. Sometimes people were like that, they would entertain your interest without them really being interested themselves. "What do you have in mind?"

"We're going to Kitchen and Bar, in the Wynwood Walls."

"I don't have anything to wear," Vanessa hoped that might have ended the conversation.

"C'mon, let's go. I'm sure you have *something* to wear, you always do."

"But it's raining!"

"So?"

"Ah . . ." Vanessa said, slightly irritated. She wanted to hang up the phone, but her inquisitiveness kept her engaged. She considered Rachel's proposal, not once, but a few times. After all, she *did* have a terrible week; she could use a drink and she did want to go somewhere, anywhere really. *But in the rain?*

"Vane . . . c'mon, I'll pick you up."

A sudden quiet came upon her--upon them-an ominous silence to be exact. It was brief, but it felt as if forever lasted a few minutes. Vanessa laughed, hoping to break the sudden mood shift.

"Okay, you win, but pick me up right out front," Vanessa insisted.

"Okay, bet on it."

Looking outside of her window, Vanessa hung up the phone as the rain poured and it poured hard enough, but still, she ignored the rain and she went to her bedroom to get ready.

2

It was 9:46 p.m. and the rain was non-stop, as doubt began to crowd Vanessa's thoughts.

"Maybe this is a bad idea. Maybe it's not too late to cancel," she thought. She didn't like canceling. She thought it was ridiculous. People who canceled at the last minute were such a burden to keep around and she never wanted to be a burden.

The phone rang.

"I'm out front," Rachel said.

"Okay, let me grab my umbrella and I'll be right there."

"Okay, bet."

Vanessa hated when Rachel would say, "bet." She didn't understand what it meant, but no one did, and no one cared-except for Vanessa.

Vanessa walked out with a lime-green raincoat and a see-through umbrella decorated with little black dots. Rachel was in her black BMW 328i. It was so dark and dismal outside that the headlights were the only things you could see. The rain was like a war tour in the Middle East: violent and relentless. It brutally slammed against the pavement and everything in its path. Doubt once again swept through Vanessa, but her friend was right in front of her. The car beeped as the window slowly rolled down.

"Hurry up! Get in!"

Rachel sounded like a sergeant howling at a private to do something he didn't want to do. Vanessa opened the door and without thinking it over, jumped into the car. Barely wet from the rain, she still wasn't sure if this was a good idea.

"You made it!" said Rachel as she stepped on the gas.

"Barely. You owe me big time for this," said Vanessa. Rachel laughed and smiled.

Rachel was one of *those* girls. If things didn't go as she planned, then she would throw a fit. If you did otherwise, she would turn into a different person and it was one you didn't want to get caught in the middle with. She would always talk her way into things and out of them well.

3

Typically a 15-minute drive, it took close to 45 minutes to get to Wynwood. The rain had made the crazy drivers even crazier.

"I hate how everyone drives so slowly. I mean yes, it's raining, but come on, twenty miles an hour? I could jog faster than that," Rachel complained.

They both decided to valet the car and drove to a garage attached to the bar. They did this to avoid the rain, for neither of them wanted to walk into a bar wet.

Rachel pulled in and rolled her window down.

"How much is it for the night?"

"$20.00 all night," the valet replied.

Rachel pulled out a $20 from her purse and handed her keys along with the money to the valet.

"Okay, let's go," she said to Vanessa.

Vanessa checked her makeup in the rearview mirror. She fluffed her hair, reapplied lipstick, and pouted her lips. Satisfied, she grabbed her purse and opened the car door.

When they finally set foot in the bar, it was packed: the weird people, the business people, and the ones who drank all night. People of all types would come here to relax and ease off a little.

As if they had wings, the girls soared on over to grab their first drink. Rachel tapped a guy blocking their way.

"Excuse me, can you move so my friend and I can order a drink?"

"You need a drink?" he asked with a half-empty bottle of Corona in his hand and a large cigar in the other.

"No, I need you to move over so I can order," Rachel yelled to be heard over the music. She could barely hear herself.

"Oh, okay." He moved to the side and she waited in the line until the bartender noticed her.

"Can I get you something?" The bartender leaned over the counter to place empty glasses into the sink.

"Yes, two Pinot Grigios!" Rachel yelled--the music seemed to get louder and louder. Vanessa just stood behind Rachel as she ordered.

4

A while later, they were both four to five wine glasses in.

"I feel great," said Vanessa, sitting on a bar stool close to a table.

"Yeah, me too. I needed this, it's been hectic lately, especially at work," Rachel replied.

"Yes, same here. Sometimes I just want to get my stuff and quit--and not just work but other things as well. Sometimes I just want to pick up my things and go and I don't know where to, but just go, somewhere different you know? Things can get so stressful around here. It's not easy."

"Yeah, stress. We'd all like to quit," said Rachel as she took a gulp of wine.

"Holy shit!" Vanessa said, suddenly cowering halfway beneath the table.

"Oh my god, you *are* drunk! Get up from there, girl," said Rachel.

"No I can't," Vanessa muttered.

"Why not?"

"Because I just saw *him*!"

"Saw who?" Rachel scanned the room. She tried to figure out who Vanessa was talking about.

"I see a lot of people. Who are you talking about, Vane?"

"Jake!"

"Holy shit! He's *here*?" said Rachel as she cowered under the table next to Vanessa.

"Yes!" said Vanessa.

BEAUTIFUL AND DAMNED

Rachel slowly came up from beneath the table to see exactly where he was.

"Oh shit! Oh, my god! He *is* here!" said Rachel.

"Where is he now? Don't let him see me!"

Stack on another problem besides the rain. Jake was Vanessa's long-lost boyfriend. They had been together for almost five years and then suddenly it just ended-- without explanation, without a reason. It just ended. No phone call, no email, no text message, nothing. It was as if he had just disappeared.

It had been about five months since that nightmare had happened. Vanessa had been devastated. And now, seeing him rattled her confusion more than ever. She froze--even after all the conversations, the reenactment, and the role-playing that occurred in her head, that is, if she ever ran into him--she already knew what to say. And she did, indeed, have so much to say, and now, finally, the love of her life was across the room and her mind went blank. She couldn't find the courage to go up to him. It was as if all of that elevating fire she had contained within her for so long dissipated in that very moment. Seeing him after five long months made her want to break down and cry, but she refused to give in and held strong. She held it in as if her life depended on it.

"Girl, get up from there," said Rachel.

Vanessa charged up enough courage, took a deep breath, and sat back up on the stool.

"If he sees you, act like he doesn't matter to you. Be strong; that's what I'd do. Make it known that you're okay, because you are. You're okay and I'm here with you," said Rachel.

Vanessa silently looked at Rachel and had this look in her eyes as if she knew what to do in the event of him noticing her.

"You're right. Forget it. It's not like *I* did anything wrong. I mean *he's* the one that ruined everything. He ruined me; he ruined us. He left and I stayed. I waited and maybe I waited too long, but nonetheless, I waited. But he never came back."

"He didn't ruin you, Vane. You're stronger now. Sometimes life throws these types of things at you. Look at yourself. You're doing well. I mean, sure you freaked out a little, but overall, you've got this."

"Yes! I've got this! Let's order another round."

"Okay," said Rachel as she motioned for the waiter. She asked for two more glasses of Pinot Grigio and then two more--as the night went on, as the rain went on, and as she and Rachel went on toward the mystery of the night.

5

By midnight, Vanessa was ready to go home. She wasn't tired. She wasn't bored. She just didn't want to run into Jake. She kept seeing him pass by from afar and every time she saw him, her heart would stop for a few seconds and slowly come back to reality. She didn't know how to handle all of this--really, no one ever does. All she knew was when he passed by, a wringing sensation came from the center of her body and she would slowly feel a sting.

Rachel, on the other hand, was pissed drunk. She wasn't a bad drunk; she kept her cool and posture. A little alcohol didn't faze her; the way she came in was the way she'd go out. Hell, by the way she drank, you would think she was a man trapped in a woman's body.

"I have to pee, come with me to the bathroom," said Rachel as she struggled to get off the stool.

"Okay," Vanessa said, putting her glass down, grabbing her purse, and scanning the room to make sure Jake wasn't around.

As they passed through the crowd, Vanessa noticed Jake with a group of friends. He was such a socialite. People always flocked around him. Laughter would follow wherever he went. Vanessa kept walking, but her eyes never lost his location. Again, she didn't know what to feel. She only had that sick sensation in her gut and it kept growing. And then, she had a moment, as all people do before they break and shatter. For the first time, she felt as if she had enough courage to talk to him but she didn't. Instead, she waited for Rachel, outside the restroom. In the meantime, her phone vibrated. She grabbed it and noticed two unread messages and when she saw who they were from, she was, at first, taken aback, but at the same time, she felt relatively calm.

The first text:

"Hey . . ."

The second text:

"You left already? Without saying hi or goodbye?"

Her heart pounded and it pounded hard. A cold chill ran through her. It was Jake. She wanted to write back, but she had too much pride. So she did what all hurt people would have done and do. She ignored everything and placed her phone back into her purse.

"Ready?" said Rachel as she jetted from the bathroom.

"Yes," said Vanessa with her face incomplete and her body as stiff as a board.

"What's up? Are you okay?"

"No, not really. I'm not--"

"What happened, Vane? Did you run into him?"

"Well, no . . . I mean, yes . . . I mean, I don't know . . ." Said Vanessa as a thousand different feelings rushed into her body all at once. The girls walked back to the bar to pay their tab and as they got closer, Vanessa felt a light tug on her shirt.

It was Jake. She froze, but it wasn't noticeable. She wanted to crawl into the depths of her own skin. She wanted to scream yet sing. She wanted him, but she didn't. She was happy but filled with sorrow, broken. His smile had come back to her like the rising sun and it drew a little light upon her darkness.

"Hey . . ." His voice, the one voice that could conquer all of her demons, had arisen from the dead and it had come back to her like a penetrating boomerang collapsing whatever was left of her world. She wanted to fall all over him, but in an instant, she remembered. She remembered a little too well--what he had done to her-yet she had been so numb that she had almost forgotten what it was all about, what had happened.

"So, you're not going to talk to me?"

She wanted to talk, but the words didn't come out; they *couldn't* come out. It was as if she had built a wall many moons ago. A wall to prevent her from ever talking to him, but none of that mattered.

"Yes?" Vanessa replied. Her face was cold and emotionless as she watched him flash his convincing smile.

"Come on . . . is that all you got?" Jake replied.

"I don't know what you expect me to say." Vanessa looked back at Rachel. Rachel had no words for her friend, for him, or for the situation. She isolated herself from the two. She was close enough to hear but far enough not to get involved.

"Well, I just wanted to say hi, and I wanted to tell you that you look beautiful tonight . . . and . . . that I'm sorry . . . for everything . . . and I'm sorry for all the trouble I might have caused."

"Okay . . . thank you . . ." said Vanessa. She tried to create a moat around her heart, to no avail.

"Okay . . . I'll get going now . . . have a goodnight, V."

Jake quickly turned away but deep within him, he, too, felt something, but it wasn't the sick feeling Vanessa had felt, no, it wasn't that. It was far worse. He was torn, filled with regret, so much regret that it almost made him immobile, but he did manage to walk through the exit, out into the rain, and all she could do was to watch him go and all he did was watch her stay behind, as he walked out the door with her heart in his hands, and there was nothing she could do beyond that.

6

It came suddenly, like a fast push off an edge. From the moment he walked away, something within Vanessa clicked and without thought, as if struck by a miracle, she ran outside and into the rain.

"Vane! Where are you going?" Rachel yelled as she saw Vanessa rush out after Jake.

Vanessa stumbled across a few people standing at the entrance and knocked someone's umbrella to the ground.

"Sorry!" she shouted, looking for Jake. She saw him about half a block away with his hands in his pockets. He didn't care it was raining. She ran toward him and stopped a few feet away from him. The wind whispered as she charged herself up.

"Why did you go?" she yelled as Jake turned around to look her in the eyes. He walked toward her and stopped a few inches away.

Rain splattered on Vanessa, but she didn't even notice. "Why did you leave me? What did I do?" The only word that made sense to Vanessa when he left her, the only word she had repeatedly said to herself for the past five months was "why?"

"Just tell me why?" Vanessa continued, wiping the rain from her brow. "I have been beating myself up over you . . . I thought you were happy, I thought I was happy; I thought we were happy . . . just tell me why?" Both of them felt that they needed each other to pick themselves back up. She began to tear and she couldn't stop, it couldn't stop. She just kept on crying. She hated this because she had lost all self-control. She didn't want to be seen like this, especially by him. Maybe it was the alcohol, she thought, but she didn't care. She was out of her mind, out of her heart, out in the rain, and all she wanted was a way back in.

"Something happened to me," he said.

"Something you wouldn't understand." Jake wiped the rain from his face. "You think it was easy for me to leave you behind? You were the only person that understood me." Said Jake, as Vanessa stayed silent.

The coldness of the rain ran down his face and an unexplainable sadness filled him. When it came to things like this, he was the one to avoid confrontation at all cost, but he did feel as if he owed an explanation to Vanessa.

But at this moment, she didn't care what had happened. She only cared about what was going on now. She just wanted to collapse into his arms like that first time they locked eyes so many years before.

"I didn't want to hurt you . . . and every night, for the past five months, I've been beating myself up, too," Jake muttered. I've been fighting with myself, trying to reason with myself, and hoping to give myself the courage to come back for you."

"*Come back for me*?"

"Yes, I mean, eventually I would have . . ."

"But why? Why did you go? Why didn't you take me with you?"

"I had to go. I had to do it for me. I felt like I was missing something in my life. I was searching for myself, for something, a clue--anything to make me feel complete again. I went to several places and met different people. And yes, it was a good experience, but every night, alone in my bed, all I could do was wonder, wonder about you. Everything, every moment, every person and every place, all of it has led me back to you and it has always been all for you. It will always be you!"

"Did you find what you were looking for?"

"No I didn't, but I'm here now, and so are you and here we are, together again, within this moment, beneath the rain . . ." He glanced at Vanessa. They both understood each other and there was not much either one could say. She was hurt and so was he and neither of them knew what was going on--not exactly. All they knew was this moment and in this very moment, they felt at peace. They even felt something that reminded them of their love.

7

The next day, the sun broke through Vanessa's bedroom curtains. She lay in bed for a few moments thinking about Jake-about what happened the night before. She felt as if a weight had been lifted off her shoulders. And it felt good, at least good enough for her to get up and face the day. Her phone vibrated and she saw one unread message:

"I've missed you."

It was from Jake. The waves within her were calm and the breeze in her heart was a smooth sail. She took a deep breath and felt alive. She felt better about herself and her life. She let herself go as she burned with desire and never looked back, the same way lovers never look back. And she knew things were about to change but for the best. She had a good feeling. And like all things that were worth it, she took a chance and wrote back, and she did it without regret, without hurt, and without her guard up.

"I've missed you too."

THE JOURNEY

1

He wore a light brown trench coat and an old black hat. The hat was probably older than he was. His briefcase, as always, was filled with papers from his business trip.

The train finally stopped. He had been on it for nearly five hours and was finally arriving home. Sometimes business would take him away for a few days and then there were longer trips that took him away two weeks at a time. He never traveled unless it was for business. He had been an entrepreneur most of his life and most of his life he had been chasing a dream, a difficult one, but ultimately a dream he hoped, one day, to conquer.

He took a few steps off the train. It had been a long and quiet ride back home--too long. The kind of ride that would inspire people to chat with each other, but there was no one to talk to. Not a single soul, just him, a briefcase, his coat, and hat. The station was even more desolate. It looked as if it hadn't been in service for several years.

He kept walking to the nearest bus stop and when he finally arrived, it too was empty-no one but the fog and the whispers of a starry night. He sat at the bus stop and waited for the bus.

"All aboard!" called the bus driver as he opened the door. It was an older bus with torn seats. Chipped paint anointed the frame. The bus driver, on the other hand, didn't look too bad. He was older, perhaps a gentleman in his late 50s.

The man got on, paid the toll, and grabbed a seat in the middle. Except for the driver, the bus was empty. He didn't think anything of it. Sometimes there aren't enough people in different towns, and he, being a man of business and travel, knew that some towns were small and ghostly.

He rang the bell to notify the driver that the next stop was his. The driver pulled to a stop. The man got off and walked the rest of the way home.

When he reached his front door, things looked as if he'd never left. He opened the door and walked in. The lights, the air conditioner, almost everything in the home was off. Tired from the trip, he turned everything back on and went upstairs. It was nearly 10 p.m. it was

well past his bed time but tonight he just couldn't
sleep there was too much going on in his mind.

He entered his room. There was a bed, a table, and a
chair facing the window. He sometimes would open the
window and just stare outside for no reason whatsoever.
What he was looking for, he didn't know. It seemed as
if he was always waiting for something to happen,
something that would give him a story to tell.

He cracked the window open and sat in the chair. He
grabbed his book and spent the rest of his evening
reading and enjoying the rest of the night.

2

Later that night, while engrossed in a new chapter,
a black bird flew straight into his room. As if it were
running from a predator, it made a commotion. The man
scanned the room for the bird. He wanted to help it
find the window so it would fly back out and let him
get back to his reading. The bird clamored from behind
the man's briefcase. After moving a few things around,
he finally found the bird lying on the floor.

"Eh, you . . . am I dead?" the bird said.

Astonished that the bird spoke, the man almost lost
his balance.

"What? Excuse me? Did you--"

"Just talk? Yeah, I did. Now, can you tell me if I'm dead? Am I still alive?" The bird was laying on its back with its wings open and its feet up towards the air.

The man got closer to the bird and said,

"I think you're alive, barely, but yes, you look alive. How come you could hear me?" he asked.

"Hear you? Maybe you are hearing me, have you ever thought about it like that? By the way, do you happen to have a cigarette? I really need one. It will help me get out of this funk." The bird sat upright and fluffed its feathers.

"This funk?"

"Yeah, I had a run in with the misses, so I took a stroll and ended up here. You know, sometimes you aren't paying enough attention to things and you end up in strange places."

He thought the bird had a point. Sometimes you get so caught up in your own life that you barely have any control where you end up. You barely know what's going on and you barely understand why such events happen, that is, if you weren't paying close attention.

"I get you, and no, I don't have a cigarette. I
don't smoke."

"Well, how about something to eat? I'm a bit
hungry."

"No, my refrigerator is empty; I just got home from
a long trip and I'm a bit tired."

"Tired? Have you gone mad? But there's so much to
do, how could you possibly be tired?"

"Working will do that to you and no I have not gone
mad, at least not yet. But I *am* talking to you. So
perhaps, I am mad. Or maybe all of this is nothing more
but a dream? I have been having a lot of strange dreams
lately."

"No, I don't think so; this doesn't feel like a
dream. It feels real and now that you confirmed that I
am not dead, I feel very much alive. Wouldn't you
agree?" said the bird.

The man didn't say anything; he just walked toward
his bed. He wasn't afraid, perhaps a bit confused, but
he was too tired to try to make sense of what was going
on.

"I have a great idea," said the bird as he flew to
the bed, next to his pillow.

"And what would that be?" the man replied.

"Let's get some food," the bird suggested.

"Get some food? I'm too tired. Anyway, I don't own a car."

"*You don't own a car*?" The bird gave his wings a good stretch as he fanned them out.

"No, I ride a bicycle everywhere, is that so hard to believe?"

"Okay, well then let's get going on the bicycle," the bird quipped.

"You're a bird; you could just fly there."

"That is quite true, but like you, I am, too, a bit too tired to flap these sleepy wings. Can't you do me this favor? I mean, your wall did crash into me."

"Is that so?"

"Yes, it is so. What do you say?" The bird separated two feathers with his beak.

The man didn't want to go, but something inside of him insisted that he do it.

"What do you have in mind, little black bird?"

"I have just the place. Let's go. By the way, what do they call you, mister?"

"My name is Peter," he said as he got up from the bed and headed for the door.

"Peter? Okay, got it." The bird gave a light chirp. "My friends call me Chuck." The bird followed Peter downstairs.

"Nice to meet you, Chuck. Shall we get going?"

"Yes, I'll tell you where, just listen to my directions."

They left Peter's house in search of something appetizing to eat. As far as the bird was concerned, the night was young and without hesitation, the bird led the rest of the way.

3

"Right here, this is the place."

They stopped in front of a store. It was dead quiet- -no cars, no security, just the two of them and the eerie blackness of the sky.

"Riley's Pet Store? Are you serious? There's nothing for me to eat in there," said Peter.

"Yes, I know that. We can go here first and then we'll fetch you something after."

"But it's closed . . . and I'm not going to wait here all night. I do have things to attend to tomorrow morning. I'm a very busy man."

"I think you have a point there, Peter. Let me think."

"Okay, I'm going home," Peter said as he grabbed the handlebar on his bicycle and hopped back on.

"No, wait, let me think, there must be something we can do," the bird chirped.

"There is nothing we can do. It's closed."

"Wait! There is," the bird squawked.

"No, believe me there isn't. We'd have to break in," Peter said with a slight grunt.

"Great idea, Peter, I *knew* you were a smart human."

"No, there is no way we are doing that, are you crazy?"

"Well, *you're* the one talking to a bird."

"Well that doesn't help much now does it?"

"No it doesn't," said Chuck as he flew around the store to see if the coast was clear.

"There's no one in sight. No one will even notice."

"No, Chuck, that's out of line. I'm going home."

"Okay. Okay. Wait . . ."

Chuck flew closer to the back entrance and noticed the back door had been left slightly ajar.

"Come back here; I think I've just found a solution to my dilemma, to *our* dilemma."

On a whim, Peter followed Chuck to the back to see what he was going on about.

"*That's* how we are going to get in," said Chuck, first flying close to the door and then landing on Peter's shoulder.

"That's still breaking and entering."

"Not if it's already open." Chuck replied smugly. "Let's say we *accidentally* stumbled inside and *accidentally* took some Mazuri: the best parrot food in the business. It will be quick--by the time you're in, you'll be out. Trust me; I've done this before with other people."

169

"Parrot food? But you're not a parrot, Chuck," said
Peter as he stood before the partially opened door. He
contemplated going in, or better yet, the consequences
of going in.

Peter looked at the door. Maybe it wasn't such a bad
idea; maybe it would be over in a flash. Maybe he
wasn't too crazy for doing all of this. He had been
living in such a bubble and felt if he did do this; it
might bring some excitement back into his life--even if
it did last only a few moments.

"Okay, I'll do it."

"Okay, it's Mazuri . . . it's a blue box. All I need
is one box, got it?"

"Yeah, I got it," Peter whispered as he snuck in
through the door.

4

With his courage on his sleeve, Peter grabbed the
door lever and without thinking twice, he pushed the
door and went inside. Of course, like all pet shops,
there were other animals inside, caged. Some slept
soundly, while others were wide awake and watched Peter
sneak across the store.

"It's right over there . . . on the shelf in front of you," Chuck yelled from the door. *So much for stealth*, thought Peter as he went through with the plan.

Peter felt good. He felt dangerous. He wanted to feel this way everyday as if he was living on the edge of the sun. *Everyone deserved this type of life*, he thought as he went for the parrot food. But then, something happened. Something that was not meant to happen, something neither Chuck nor Peter could have anticipated.

Peter couldn't think because the flashing lights and the sirens were too loud. Four cop cars rushed the entrance and another two rushed the back. Scared, Peter did something even more unexpected, something he thought he would have never been able to do. He took off and ran out of the store with the parrot food on his hand, but of course, it didn't work. The cops pointed their guns at him and yelled.

"Get down on the ground!"

Peter stopped, dropped the parrot food and put his hands on the air.

"You are going to get it, mister," some cop yelled as another one rushed toward Peter and tackled him onto the pavement.

"You're under arrest!" The cops quickly cuffed him, picked him up, and slammed him into the back of the cop car. Peter didn't know what to feel or think. Maybe this is all just one giant nightmare. Was he being rushed to the station for questioning? He tried to remain calm, but it was very hard, considering the circumstance. He had never been to jail. He had always lived a decent life. All he did was work and work some more. He never had any time for himself; in fact, he wasn't even sure if he knew himself. All he knew was he was about to go to jail for something he didn't even want to do to begin with.

"It was the bird's idea, officer, and the door was open. I was going in to get him some parrot food, that's all. Can't I just be let off with a warning?" Peter asked the officer.

"I'm sure you're a good person, you're *all* good people," said the cop.

"What's *that* supposed to mean? Are you patronizing me, officer?"

"Look, you broke into a store and for goddamn who knows what. I'm taking you in. The judge will decide what to do with you in the morning and that's it!" said the cop as he drove through a red light.

"You just took the red!" said Peter.

"Around here we do whatever we want, to whoever we want, and you sir, didn't see anything."

Peter had given up and for the rest of the ride, he didn't say much. He did, however, regret what he had done; no matter how exciting it might have been and felt. He wished he had never run into Chuck or listened to his constant chatter. And so, from a train to a bus to the back of a cop car the minutes flew. Peter looked out the window as if he would never see the world again.

5

Locked in a jail cell, waiting for them to process his arrest, Peter felt a familiar feeling as he sat on a bench. It was the same solitude he had felt when he departed from the train, the bus, and when he arrived at home, and he waited as this feeling of emptiness consumed him.

Soon after, a tapping sound came from the other side of the wall. It was a small sound, lower than any other sound he had heard before. He got up and slowly walked toward the light tapping. The cops on the other side were too busy to even notice Peter snooping around his cell.

"Hey Peter, it's me, Chuck," the bird whispered. I'm going to break you out, you hear me?" a muffled voice came from the wall; it sounded as if it was underwater. Peter could barely make sense of the words.

"Chuck, is that you?" Peter quietly asked.

"Yeah, it's me."

"I'm going to break you out, okay?"

"How in the hell do you expect to do that?" Peter asked as his eyes rolled to the back of his skull and he swallowed his tongue.

"Come on now, Peter, I'm full of surprises. Just wait here. I'll do the rest."

"Just wait here," Peter mumbled. "As if I could head out for a walk." Peter sat back down on the bench. What could that bird do to break him out of jail? The walls had to be at least two feet thick, concrete and bricks, and the bird must weigh about a pound. The time passed until suddenly, the lights went out. The entire police department had lost power.

"What now, what can possibly go wrong now?" Peter said to himself as he waited for Chuck to do something.

There was a loud chatter, a series of sounds, and cops' voices coming from the other side of the wall. Some of them bickered about the power outage.

"Okay, extend your hands Peter, here's the key, use it," Chuck demanded as he placed a keys onto Peters hands. "You've got about 30 seconds before the emergency lights come on, so hurry."

Peter grabbed the keys and fiddled with the lock.

"Hurry up, will you!" urged Chuck from the vast darkness of the cell.

"I'm trying," said Peter as the keys fell to the ground.

"Shoot, I can't see the lock. I can't find it."

"Well, hurry up," Chuck snapped. "I can't open this door for you; only you can do that."

Peter pointed the key toward the black space as if he were looking for something that didn't exist, something that was meant to be there but had never been built. And then a loud click snapped.

"I got it! I did it!" Peter whispered as he opened the jail cell and tiptoed out. The commotion from the other side was going strong, but none of them ever got up, not even to check on Peter. As they kept ranting, Peter smoothly sailed through the door and ran as fast and as far as he could.

"That was close," said Chuck, landing on Peter's shoulder.

"Yeah, it was." Peter slowed down to catch his breath.

"So, what now?" asked Chuck.

"What do you mean? Look at the trouble you got me into. I'm getting the hell away from you."

"I don't think you mean that. I mean, look what has happened tonight. We met by accident. I gave you a little fire, a little life, and you seemed like you needed something like this to happen. You should be thanking me, pal. Don't be ungrateful."

"No I don't think so," said Peter as he continued home. He looked up at the sky and thought maybe tonight was one of the best nights of his life. It was risky, reckless, and not far beyond immature, but it did indeed get the blood in his body going.

"You know this would have had never happened if you hadn't crashed into my wall," Peter said.

"I think you're right, but I also believe you're wrong. I mean yes, your wall did crash into me while I was out taking a stroll, so that makes you wrong, but, and I rarely admit this, you are right about one thing," said chuck.

"And what might that be?"

["How some things are meant to happen and how some things aren't and how both of them are for a reason. No matter what happens, it is all always for a reason. And I think we met for a reason or maybe we didn't. I wouldn't know."]

6

"Hello and welcome to your first day at the Neurodevelopmental Disorders Clinic. We are excited to have our new nurses with us today," said Miss June, a senior RN. "Let's take a tour of the clinic and introduce you to some of our in-house patients," Miss June said as she grabbed her files and clipboard.

There were at least five floors in the clinic and each floor had a main hall, a guest lobby, and twenty patient rooms. The new nurses followed Miss June around the entire building, greeting some of the other employees, and meeting some of the patients as well.

As they continued to walk, they came across room 412. Miss June quietly opened the door.

"Peter, there's some people here to meet you."

Sitting in a chair, facing the window, sat an older man wearing a light brown trench coat and an old black hat. The hat was probably older than him. His briefcase sat next to him on the floor, empty.

"This is Peter, he's autistic, and he has been here for several years. He never moves and never says a word, poor thing; I wonder what goes through his mind."

Peter sat there as if nothing was going on upstairs, as if he had gone away, and had never returned.

"Well, come now; let me show you the rest of the patients. You'll be working with several of them on this floor."

Miss June closed Peter's door and the nurses continued with the tour.

As the door closed, something happened, something out of the ordinary. A little black bird crashed toward Peter's window. It barely survived but still, the bird managed to shake itself off. The bird began to tap on the window as if it had an urgent message to deliver.

Then, Peter lifted his finger and placed it toward the bird's tapping beak as if they shared a long-kept secret, one that the world was never meant to know. For a moment, Peter kept his finger on the window as the bird lightly tapped. And then, they both looked toward the sky and Peter smiled and smiled hard enough he did, because deep down inside, he knew the bird understood his story and he understood the bird's story.

And with a fair exchange both Peter and the bird took off and they were never to be found from that day on, for they both had drifted to a place where only little black birds and older men gather and it was a place where only the beautiful and the damned were welcomed.

[Everything starts right now and if it doesn't,
then leave it, something better is on its way]

ROBERT M. DRAKE

ON THE EDGE

1

I worked all day, about 12 hours. I did that almost every day. Monday through Saturday and Sundays, I was usually too tired to do anything. I was a mechanic. All day, I worked on the same beat-up cars, doing the same beat-up job, for the same beat-up people. My god, was this the life we all were promised?

Today, like all days, I left for home late. When I started my engine, the car shook in violent rattles. It was cold outside and the heater in my car was shot. I rolled all my windows up and lit my last cigarette to warm myself as the engine heated up.

I took a few tokes off my cigarette and rubbed my hands together as the vapors from my breath filled the car and the windows began to fog. I wiped them down, but it was too foggy outside to see. Then, my car just shuts off. This goddamn piece of metal junk always failed on me. I took one last toke off my cigarette, climbed out of the car, and popped the hood. Damn alternator froze up. I walked back inside the shop to grab something to get the car cranking. I replaced it

with a rebuilt alternator, but it didn't start, nothing
worked and hell, it was getting late.

"I could always take the bus home and figure it out
in the morning," I thought. I only lived 15 minutes
away and it wasn't too much of a wait to catch a bus.
(It wasn't the first time either.) I waited by the bus
stop and damn; it was so cold, I couldn't stand it. It
was a good thing there was a small bar and lounge
across the street. I walked towards the bar and I went
inside to get a pack of cigarettes. Except for the
bartender, the place was empty.

"Can I offer you a drink?"

"No, I'm just here to get a pack of cigarettes from
the vending machine."

"Well, come on over. One drink won't hurt. It's on
the house," he insisted. Stressed about my car, I went
ahead and took that offer. There weren't many times I
was offered a free drink.

"What will it be?" the bartender asked as he wiped a
glass and placed it on the table.

"Give me vodka with tonic water."

"Okay, coming right up."

He poured the drink so eloquently that you'd think this was the last drink he would ever make--such graceful skill, it was almost too beautiful to bear. I grabbed the glass.

"Thanks, I'm going to need this."

"I know you are." He chuckled a little.

"What do you mean?" I asked.

"Well, let's just say I feel you. I mean, look at the bad weather and you're just getting out of your job now. It must be a little frustrating for you."

"Yeah and on top of everything else, my damn car broke down."

"Yeah. I know," he said.

I took another gulp from my drink.

"What do you mean you know? You saw me out there?"

I took another gulp.

"No," he said. "I just happen to know things about you. Some things you don't even know about yourself. Should I pour you another drink?" He grabbed another glass and wiped it. I didn't agree on another drink, but he poured it anyway. I was a little boggled out, but I had such a terrible week, that honestly, another drink wouldn't hurt, plus this guy had me intrigued, there was something gravitational about him.

"Now, listen, I don't know you. We have never met, so I think you're confusing me with someone else," I muttered.

"No, there's no confusion here. You're Jason Mekenzie. You're 38 years old and you hate your life. You feel that everyone is out to get you and that's why you work all day. That's why you feel so alone sometimes. You think no one cares and you feel as if no one will ever care. I know you're miserable and that sometimes you think the unthinkable, but I want you to know, you're not alone, people do care, and there is always someone here to help you. Believe me, I know."

I stumbled--the stool fell over me and the glass shattered all over the floor. I was speechless. *Who was this guy? And how did he know so much about me? What the hell was going on here?*

The bartender went around and with a gentle smile, he reached out and gave me his hand. I was confused, but nonetheless, I reached for the lending hand. He looked me in the eyes as he helped me up, smirked slightly, and then came close enough to whisper in my ear.

"Don't you recognize me, Jason? Have you forgotten about me? You used to talk to me every night as a child but as you got older, you became so distant of me. Jason, don't you know who I am? Don't you know how much I worry about you, think about you, and love you? Jason, you are everything to me."

"Who are you?" I asked.

"Jason, I'm God..." he slowly said as this unexplainable warmth flushed through me, flooding my hurting chest. I was no longer cold. I felt different, but a good different, strange, but a good strange.

"*God?*"

"I've been watching you. I'm here with you. You are not alone; you have never been alone. And I want you to know that I know how much you hate yourself and your life, but Jason, listen to me. You are so precious and delicate. You are golden and it hurts me to watch you drag your life into this bottomless darkness when you are loved by so many. You don't see it, but I do. I see everything."

"Everything?"

"Yes, everything. I need you to do something for me, Jason. I need you to believe in yourself the way I believe in you. I need you to find the beauty in everything and I need you to be who you once were.

Remember, Jason. Remember me and you will never feel
the bitterness again. That I promise to you. Could you
do that for me?"

This is what it felt like to have your soul break
and then put back together by someone who cared. I felt
his love rush through my veins and it pulled me closer
while it pushed me further apart and it was beautiful.
He was beautiful and everything about him lived within
me. I could feel it.

"Yes, I can."

"I know you can. I'm God, remember? Now wake up.
Wake up, Jason . . . you're okay."

"Jason, are you okay? Jason wake up. Wake up, Jason,
wake up. . ."

2

My boss shook me. I was inside of my car, in the
same position I was when I first got in after work. The
engine was on and my last cigarette was still between
my fingers, unlit.

"What happened? Where am I?" I asked.

"Nothing happened, I just saw you get inside of your
car and then you just dozed off the moment you got

inside of it. You've been working a lot. Take a couple days off. You need it," my boss said, patting me on the back.

"Yeah, I think so. Well, I got to go. I'll call in the morning to see if you need me."

I pulled away from the curb and passed by the bar, the same bar I had just dreamt about. I had this urge to go inside-to see if all of this was just my imagination. I mean as ridiculous as it sounded, I just had to go inside and check it out myself.

I parked my car, closed the door, and walked into the bar. There were several people, many of them smoking and drinking, but the bar was unattended. I looked around for that same bartender but he couldn't be found. I searched profusely and nothing, no luck.

What a dream, I thought as I walked out of the bar.

"Sir! Your wallet!"

A young man ran toward me with my wallet in his hand. As he got closer, his face looked familiar. It was the bartender from my dream. He was just a regular guy, having a regular night, in a regular bar.

"Here you go, sir, this is yours. You left it at the bar."

"Thank you, this happens to me all the time," I said as he handed me my wallet.

"I hear you; you are not alone," he replied. "You have never been alone." He gave me a wink, a smile, and threaded back into the bar.

[And that's when I knew . . .

How sometimes you find God in the most unusual places and sometimes he reveals himself in the most surprising ways.

And at that moment, I was reminded how I was always with someone. And how somewhere, there was always someone looking out for me. No matter how far I went and no matter how close I got to it all.]

THE MAN IN THE RAT MASK

1

Thirsty, I went downstairs to grab a drink. I lived in a two-story house so it was quite the walk, nineteen steps, two hallways, five bedrooms, three living rooms, two kitchens, and a yard the size of a small South American country. No one lived within a two-mile radius, at least not yet. There was a lot of construction here and not many people had bought the houses being built nearby. I had been living here for about four months. It was my wife, our two-month-old baby, and myself. Most nights, the baby would be kicking up a storm, but not tonight--tonight was different. She was put to bed around 8 p.m. and only woke to feed.

It was just after one in the morning. I made my way downstairs and turned on the kitchen light. It was a low, dimmed ambient glow, the kind that filled the heart with warmth and gentleness. I grabbed an empty cup, opened the refrigerator, and poured ice water. I sat on the couch, checked my social media to see if any friends had messaged, but no one had. I didn't think much of it. I knew I was the only one up at this hour. I didn't work and to be honest, for the life of me, I couldn't say when the last time was that I had a real job. I had inherited some money a few years ago, and it was quite enough, more than enough. My mother had a life insurance policy and on top of that, a lot of investments in Apple, Inc. Who would have guessed, she had about 110,000 shares and they were all well worth $700.00 at that time. Sadly, my mother passed away. She left me with all of it and with the money I bought this house, two cars, and had a baby. I didn't know what to do with the rest of it, so I put most of the funds in an IRA.

It was about an hour later and I was thinking about the things I had to do throughout the upcoming day. My wife and I had a strict routine. We would wake up, take the baby for a walk, and eat breakfast at the local coffee shop right across the street. After that, we did whatever we wanted to do, although most days, we didn't do much. We just stayed home and worked on the house, while other days we had so much on our plate, we barely had time for anything else: Not to eat. Not to talk. Not to live.

I was about ready to go back upstairs, not to sleep, but to read the online paper in bed. I turned off the kitchen light and walked toward the stairs when suddenly I heard a breaking sound coming from one of the rooms downstairs. It wasn't loud, in fact, I barely heard it. *Maybe, it was all in my head?* I was going to let it go, but if my wife heard it, she would make me come back downstairs to be sure everything was how it should be.

I turned on the hallway light and peeped my head into the room. Of course, I wasn't scared--it was just . . . this was a new house and, you know, when you move into a new neighborhood, especially one you are not too familiar with, you begin to think things. I looked around and saw nothing. And then, in the mist, between the light, the walls, and the shadows from the curtains, I saw the image of a man. He walked out of the closet as if he had been searching for something. My first thought was to grab my pistol but it was upstairs. I'd probably make too much noise running up there--I didn't want to wake my wife or the baby. My second thought was to ambush him but then I thought he might have a weapon--my life and my family's lives would be at risk. My final option was to talk to him and figure out why the he was in my house in the middle of the night.

Out of the three options, I had no choice but to go with the third one. So I mustered enough courage and went on with my plan.

2

He wasn't too tall, about my height, and he wore ragged jeans, as torn and old looking as if they had gone through hell and back and then returned to hell for more. He smelled funny, different, and it wasn't a good different. He also wore a black hooded sweatshirt, so my first impression was that he was a burglar. I snuck up behind him as he looked around.

"Who are you?" I asked, my voice as firm as an old oak tree.

He slowly turned and that's when I saw the beady-eyed rat mask.

"A rat mask? What the hell are you doing here? Who the hell are you?" I yelled as I turned on the lights.

He stood there motionless. Perhaps he thought I wouldn't see him if he was still. He was calm, too calm, and that made me jittery.

"You look different, from what I remember, from what I expected," he replied in a deep, muffled voice.

"What are you talking about? *Who* are you?"

"Damien, you look far younger than I thought you'd be by this time."

"How do you know my name?"

The situation went from odd to possibly dangerous. This man broke into my house, knew my name, and had probably followed my family and I for weeks--maybe even months.

"Look, I don't want any trouble. I've got nothing of value. Why don't you go home? I won't call the police and we can all pretend like nothing has happened here tonight. I mean for Christ's sake, I have a child upstairs."

The man in the rat mask stepped back and glanced furtively around the room.

"This is where you wanted to build your art room and the other four rooms you didn't know what to do with. In fact, you are still not sure why you bought such a big house," he said as he pointed things out. They weren't obvious things. How did he know? Who was this guy? He went on to say things only I would know, things only I would think, and that spooked me even more.

"Who are you? How do you know my name?"

"Do you believe in time travel, Damien?"

"Time travel? What does that have to do with anything?"

He stood dead still as if I had just offended him.

"It has *everything* to do with it and I am not going to harm you. I'm not a burglar." His eyes met mine.

"Listen carefully to what I'm about to say. I came here to warn you, to save you and your family."

"To warn me? To save us? About what and from what? And why should I believe you? I don't even know who you are," I said as I took my cell phone out. "Perhaps I could knock him out and call the police to come get him." I thought and began to dial.

"Don't call the police. There is nothing they can do for you," he said as if he could read my mind. The funny thing is, my phone's screen wasn't visible to him. How did he know who I was calling? I mean . . . maybe I was calling my brother, maybe my friend, or maybe even someone else. There wasn't any way possible for him to have known who it was I was dialing. I hung up the phone and waited to see where all of this was going.

"Damien, what time do you have?"

"It's almost 4 o'clock in the morning. Why?"

"You need to do what I say. *Now*. We can't waste time. You know the nuclear power plant that is a few miles away?"

"Yes I do," I said, trying to calm myself down. I mean, how was I supposed to react? Someone was in my house in the middle of the night. Anyone else would have shot this guy clean between the eyes, but not me. I wasn't sure why I hadn't fully reacted the way I always told myself that I would in this sort of circumstance. Sometimes things don't go as planned. No one is ever prepared for a moment like this. I mean yes, a lot of people would say "If someone ever breaks into my house they're dead," but how many people would *really* do it? It took more than tough words to shoot someone and perhaps, in some sense, I never saw myself in this type of situation, as if anyone really would. In the end, talk is cheap and it's what you do that's golden.

3

"Something terrible is about to happen. Something that will leave you in the darkness for the rest of your life," the masked man said as he took a seat. I didn't know whether to feel sorry for him or actually believe him.

"What do you mean? Where are you from? And why are you wearing that ridiculous mask?"

"None of that matters-I'm serious, there isn't much time, so please listen to me. You have to get your wife and baby away--as far as possible. There's going to be a meltdown in about 35 minutes. Everything within a five-mile radius will be flattened."

I thought he was crazy. How could he possibly have this sort of information? Maybe he wanted me out of my

house so he and his comrades could take my belongings--
anything could happen.

"A meltdown?"

"Yes, you have to go. Forget your belongings and
just go north."

I went along and played his game. I just wanted him
out and was willing to do anything to accomplish this.

"How would you know that's about to happen?"

"I've seen it. I'm from the future."

"The future? Isn't that a little far-fetched? A rat-
faced seer? If you were really from the future,
shouldn't you be stopping the people working the
graveyard shift at the power plant? Or alerting them
about it a few weeks prior? Or telling some government
authority to do something about it? I'm sorry, please
forgive me, it's just a little too hard to swallow--you
and your story."

"You are hard to convince. I could go back a week
prior. Many have tried to stop this plant from melting
down, but every time one of us has tried, it just sets
off another disaster around the world and far worse,
too, too many butterflies, far too many. Also, we are
allowed to come back within an hour span. That's it.
Any more time could be deadly for you and all of us on

the other side. Time is fragile; it's like an ocean,
one that has never seen any waves. One tiny glimpse of
wind can change it, forever. Just please go. Please.
It's our only chance," he said.

"Okay, so if I wake up my wife and baby in the
middle of the night . . . I'm not about to come back
home to an empty house am I? I mean can I have your
identification card? After all, I don't know what you
look like and I don't know anything about you. I just
need something, incase all of this goes sour."

"Just get out! Get your wife and baby and go as far
north as possible. No questions. Just do it and do it
now," he demanded. He took out his wallet and gave me
what seemed to be an ID wrapped in a sheet of paper. I
grabbed it and unfolded it to see if I could at least
catch his name, but I didn't open it fully.

"Here's a letter too," the masked man said. "Don't
open it now, open it tomorrow, believe me, it's for the
best." He spluttered again as I put everything he
handed down to me in my pocket.

"Okay, so can I trust you?" He asked. "Don't make me
come back for you, you hear? Next time, things won't be
so easy." He stood up.

"Hey, before you go. Why me? Why us?"

"Because no one else is going to save you . . . but-
-" Suddenly, several bright flashes bounced around the
room and just like that he was gone. I fell toward the
wall as my breathing labored. I didn't know what to
think. "Had I seen a ghost?" I thought as I ran
upstairs as fast as I could and woke my wife.

"Honey, let's go." In a frantic whirl, I turned on
the lights.

"Huh? What are you talking about," she said, her
voice was groggy.

"We have to go! Hurry. Get the girl. I'll explain in
the car." I was desperate and a bit frantic.

"What are you talking about, Damien? You're scaring
me."

"*Let's go now*!" I said as I grabbed a suitcase and
filled it with anything I could grab. I was afraid. I
didn't know what or where we were going but one thing
was for sure, we were not staying here.

It took us minutes to get our things and jump into
our car. We headed north where my wife's mother lived,
about 18 miles away. As we drove, I told my wife what
had happened. She thought I was losing my mind, but to
be honest, who wouldn't have thought that? The story
sounded like a nightmare. I mean, a man wearing a rat
mask telling me to leave my house in the middle of the

night then vanishing before my eyes. Yeah, that was a lot to take in, especially in the middle of the night.

We arrived within 20 minutes and we were exhausted. As soon as we got to her mother's house we just fell asleep. I figured if nothing was bound to happen, then I would have a lot of explaining to do, but that could wait till tomorrow. Right now, all I wanted to do was sleep and eventually wake up from this terrible nightmare.

4

The next day was a rude awakening, a very rude awakening to be exact.

"Honey, wake up. There's been a terrible, terrible disaster." My wife, distressed and full of tears, shook me violently.

"What happened?" I asked as I climbed out of the chair I had fallen asleep on. The baby wailed. The news was on full blast and everyone was in the living room except me.

"The power plant exploded sometime this morning. They said it destroyed everything within a 5 to 6-mile radius, including our neighborhood." My wife's tears slid toward her lips and eventually toward the ground.

BEAUTIFUL AND DAMNED

I watched her cry as I tried to catch them as they fell.

My soul sank within itself. We could have died, all of us. The masked man was the only person on my mind. He saved me. He saved us.

I went back into the room to put myself back together. I couldn't believe what was happening. My wife entered the room and saw me on the edge of the bed. I trembled with shock.

"How did you know?" my wife asked.

"I told you--remember our conversation on the drive here last night? The rat-masked man warned me. I told you, I wasn't dreaming, it really happened."

Then, I remembered my left pocket. He had given me something--a letter and his identification card. I reached to grab it and thankfully it was still there.

I opened it. I had to know who this man was . . . and then, my soul broke in two; I couldn't believe what I saw. The man's ID read Damien J. Barthanul. My name. He had my birthday and height. It was me, an older me, but me. And then I opened the letter:

"Damien, do not be afraid. I know right now you are not meant to understand this and I won't go on to explain. I am writing you this letter from the future.

I know this is going to be hard for you to take in, but
on April 12, 2120, the airfield nuclear power plant
goes off and wipes out everything within a five-mile
radius. How you, we, survived is still a mystery, but
Jody--your wife--and Candice, your baby daughter--don't
make it. And my life, your life, is never the same
after that. You are destroyed by everything that had
been taken away from you and everything you loved was
destroyed that night. I had to do something. I know by
doing so, I've risked my life and yours, but I did this
for love. For the love a man can only have for his wife
and his daughter."

"I hope by the time I get back, they're both waiting
for me. I hope Jody--your wife, my wife--is as old as
me, and I hope Candice--your daughter, my daughter--is
married with children. You have no idea how terrible it
was for me (you) to go through life without them. I
hope this pain is lifted from you, from us, by the time
I get back. I love you. Please do not mention this to
anyone. Not even your wife.

P. S. Stay strong . . . and watch your diet from now
on, you'll thank me (yourself) later."

I broke down into tears. I didn't know how to hide
them. We were alive. I didn't understand it fully, but
I was grateful. I was happy and to think, in the end, I
owed my life, our lives--to myself, who was willing to
risk everything to come back and warn me. That alone
made the rest of our lives worth living. The fact that

I, well, a future me, had gone out of his way to save
and change our lives--to be honest, there was nothing
more beautiful than that.

ALWAYS YOU

1

The trip back home was always the most warming and it didn't matter where you had gone. It could have been as simple as a trip across the street or a trek across the globe. Nothing ever compared to the feeling you would get--knowing you were finally going home, knowing you were finally going to see those familiar faces--the ones that brought so much out of you, so much more. Yes, nothing was ever better than the trip back home, the anticipation, the wait, and it sometimes felt too good to be true. Going home always gave me this feeling and it was always something magical.

I was coming back from a technology conference in San Francisco. It only lasted a day, but I simply *had* to stay longer, which I did, although even those extra days didn't soothe my yearning to be there. I already missed it. I missed the pier and the fresh Pacific air. Something about that city made me fall in love and yes, I fell a little too hard, and although I was there for only a few days, every second of it was fully lived.

BEAUTIFUL AND DAMNED

By the time I arrived home, it was already night. I always preferred night flying; it helped ease my anxiety because I didn't like heights and I connected better with the darkness. I mean, I stayed up late, I worked late, and for some odd reason, I always did everything in the middle of the night.

When the plane landed, I headed straight to Starbucks. It was the only coffee shop in the terminal. I knew it would be a long night. I had to unpack, run to the store for groceries, get my dog from the kennel, and finish a few odds and ends before 9 pm.

It was almost 10 when I got home. I had done my chores, gotten everything I needed, but as soon as I stepped foot in my house, a wall of exhaustion hit me. I turned on the radio and played light music and I put the groceries in the refrigerator. I couldn't believe I had left it this empty. Sometimes, I felt as if I was still in college. I would leave everything messy and unorganized, but that's another story.

The phone rang twice. I was in front of my turned-off television with a cold beer in one hand and my dog on my lap. The phone rang a third time. I almost didn't get it--I was tired, the kind of tired where your body wants to fall into the space of sleep but your mind is still wide awake. I drifted between those two worlds like an escaped helium balloon with a broken string.

I didn't want to get up; I didn't want to talk. I didn't want to do anything. I just wanted to sit on the couch with this cold brew and stare at the blank television screen before I went to bed. The phone rang a fourth time and I grabbed it. I felt like answering was the only option. Usually, by the fourth ring, the other side would have hung up.

"Hello?" A deep silence came from the other end. I expected it was bad news and wondered how most, but not all, late night calls were usually bad news. This, of course, was my first thought. Who else would call me at this time? Not even my mother would call me after 10.

"Hello? Is anyone there?" I demanded.

"Hey." It was a girl's voice, familiar, but I couldn't tell who it was.

"Hey . . . who's this?" I replied.

"It's me, Andy."

"Andy? Andy who?" The name didn't click.

"Samantha's Andy," she said.

Then, it hit me, and it was like a wall had come down with such force, one I couldn't run far enough from. She had said *her* name, a name I wanted to forget. A name that kept haunting my dreams still riddled with

205

nightmares. A chill ran through me and for a second, my tongue felt caught in my throat.

"Sam's Andy, oh yeah, I remember you. I haven't seen you in so long. What's up? Is everything okay?" I said. *Why was she calling me*? We weren't friends; in fact, she was just Samantha's friend, nothing more, nothing less. My first guess was that something had happened to Samantha. Every night since we broke it off had been a difficult one. I mean, I had so many questions to ask and every night I would ask myself how it all went so wrong. I wasn't sure. I think no one could have ever imagined Sam and me breaking up. That idea wouldn't have had made any sense. I mean, she was everything to me. People wouldn't have guessed we had problems, but we did, little ones, I guess a bunch of little nicks that eventually turned into one big gouge. But still, it took me many moons to finally let go. Sometimes I thought that I still hadn't fully let go, perhaps not. . . I mean look at my thoughts. My mind raced as if it drove a stolen car with no recollection of what or where the brakes were. I could already tell this call wasn't going to be good. The energy was no good and Andy's tone of voice was no good. It was just a matter of how I took things and I knew anything with the name Samantha in it was bound to be no good, that is, at least on my end.

2

"Steven died," she said before I could ask if Sam was okay.

The intense chill that rushed my body felt like tiny icicles traveling through my blood. No one ever wants to hear that someone has just died.

"Steven? Samantha's cousin?"

"Yes . . ."

"Wow . . . that's terrible. What happened to him?" It was the only thing I could say other than asking how Sam was doing.

"No one knows. He just died. He went to sleep and never woke up."

Death was never easy and what was even harder was trying to explain it to anyone involved, by that I mean friends, relatives, and acquaintances. Death was one of those things. It left a hollowness in your soul. It took you away for a few moments; it made you go numb. And then, if you were lucky enough, it brought you back down to earth, to the realization of a death. And then there were those who weren't so lucky, the ones who would never come back down, the ones who stayed in a small place with nothing to hold on to but the news of that one person dying. Those were the ones who were hard to save. Those were the ones who were lost forever, the ones who were lost in the transition between the living and the dead.

I didn't know what to say. I wasn't even sure why she was telling me. I had only met him once and it was about four years ago. I'm sure he had long forgotten who I was. I could barely remember what he looked like. And then, I said the most generic thing ever to be said about death.

"At least he died in his sleep." I couldn't believe that was the best I could come up with. I mean, there was no bright side to death, there's no coming back from it. It wasn't like a jail sentence or a fight or anything like that. It was like, *boom* you're done, you've checked out, and that was it. All you left behind were the things you loved and the people and the memories and everything that came with it. You were gone. You were gone like a fading sunset kissing the horizon. You were gone and death was never something easy to respond to with a simple comment.

She didn't reply. I never had the right thing to say at the right moment. For me, it was always the opposite.

"So when is the viewing?" I asked.

"It's tomorrow," she said.

208

"Okay, thanks for letting me know," I said, pausing.
I wanted to ask how Sam was in general and all, but I
thought maybe now wasn't the right time, but it was
never the right time. Since we had broken up, I had
occasionally run into her friends. We all hung out in
the same places and there were still friends we were
both linked to. How we both hadn't bumped into each
other face-to-face was something I couldn't even
understand. [Maybe she avoided me. Maybe she had new
places she would go to, some I didn't know about. But I
did know one thing, we weren't even friends and I hated
that. I mean, I don't know why people just can't be
friends. I don't get it. You spend all your time with
someone and then, in an instant, it is all taken away.
It all turns into nothing. You avoid each other and
that's it. You're strangers as if those moments you
both created together never happened. I hated that and
I hated that I couldn't at least know how she was
doing. All I had was hope and I hoped, wherever she
was, whoever she was with . . . I hoped she was happy
and I hoped she felt free.]

3

I was in a dilemma. I didn't want to go to the
viewing. I never liked those things. I had been to one
and I had a terrible experience. It was about two years
ago when my aunt Tessie passed away. I had nightmares
about it. It left me in shock. I must have had anxiety
for many weeks after. Since then, I swore I wouldn't go

to one again and now, here I was, in the middle of
something unpredictable, and what was worse--Sam was
involved. Someway, somehow, her name would always
appear. The moment I began to forget her, she would
arrive again and again, and where I least expected her
to. But that's how it was. I understood that. Love
wasn't easy. What was even harder was getting over
someone and what was even worse than that, was seeing
that one person you loved pass you by without saying a
word. Maybe that's why I didn't like to go out. I
feared that kind of scenario; I would see her and she
would just walk by as if I wasn't in the room. That
would hurt and it would probably hurt more then I could
ever imagine.

The next day came and I convinced myself that I
wasn't going. Why put myself through so much stress? If
I didn't want to go then I shouldn't go. I mean, I
barely knew the guy and I know that sounds awful, but
it was the truth. Thousands, if not millions, of people
die each day. Did that mean I had to attend a viewing
for everyone I had ever met? Of course not and for that
reason, I decided not to go. At the moment, it just
didn't feel right to me.

I went ahead with my day; I did what I did every
weekend. I woke up a bit later than I expected. I went
jogging. I walked my dog. I had breakfast. I did
everything I would usually do. I was out and about and
the day was bright as new, but in the back of my mind
something called for me and it wanted my blood. It

wanted my bones and my all. It kept calling my name and it didn't stop. As the seconds went by, it got louder and louder. Something was telling me to go to the viewing. To go and demand answers, to go and try to work things out with Samantha. Maybe this was a good time, in a strange way, at least to reconnect and erase this unforgiving silence we had given ourselves for the past few months. If it was killing me, and it *was* killing me, then I was sure it was probably killing her too.

As the day went on, the last time we spoke and how she told me never, ever to call her again played over and over in my mind. The funny thing was she had said this to me many times before and every time I would eventually call back. But this last time, something in me had changed. I was tired of chasing her, but nonetheless, it did bite me in the end. My pride had taken the steering wheel and I never tried to contact her. And to be frank, I wasn't sure if that was what had killed me or if it was the actual break up or the fact that she didn't try to contact me either. It was a different kind of hurting, a different kind of bleeding, and it was one that, no matter how much I attempted to hide, would eventually reveal itself.

About two hours had passed. I thought about the viewing and Samantha and finally convinced myself to go. I went to the barber to get myself groomed and right after, I went to Macy's to get something new to wear. By the time I arrived home, it was almost time to

go to the viewing. I couldn't believe what I was doing
and didn't know what I would say if I saw Samantha. I
just hoped that somewhere inside of my heart, I had
enough words for the situation, enough of me to comfort
all of her, even if it was with nothing more than a
smile.

4

I intentionally arrived at the viewing late. I
didn't want to get there early. I didn't want to stay
the entire time. And because of that, I thought being
late would be the perfect time for me to show my face.
A crowd attended the viewing. Most I had never met.
They drifted in and out of the funeral home. Some stood
outside chatting. Some were inside talking in low
tones. And some were conversing in the parking lot. You
wouldn't have guessed this was a viewing, but rather,
some kind of social endeavor. Death did that though, it
brought people together, and it brought people a little
closer.

I stood outside alone with my hands in my pockets. I
grabbed my phone to check the time; it was 11:15 pm. I
walked toward my car to grab my lighter. I needed a
smoke. I was about to go back inside to give my last
words when, for some reason, I got this strong sense
that I was going to run into Sam. There was no turning
back from this point on and it was something I

eventually had to go through. I needed that type of
closure to move on.

I burned myself with the cigarette. I wasn't sure if
my anxiety caused it or if it was seeing someone's dead
body or running into Sam. I walked inside and there was
Steven and, well, let's just say he didn't look like
the Steven I remembered. He looked heavier. His hair
was long and he was dead, stiffened by the air and
collected from the debt of life. He died in his sleep
and some will argue that's probably the best way to go,
but I don't know, in fact, watching him lay in his
coffin didn't bring anything to my mind. I didn't even
question my own mortality. There was only one thing on
my mind and it was Sam. I scanned the room but didn't
see her. *Why had I even come here*? I didn't feel
comfortable. I didn't know anyone and my lip was burned
from the damn cigarette I just smoked out front. I felt
a tap on my shoulder. I looked back and it was our
friend Paul. I was surprised to see him, for it, too,
had been too long.

"Long time," said Paul as he gave me a hug.

"Yeah, it's been too long," I replied.

We both looked at Steven's body but said nothing.
Not a word about Steven. Not a word about death and we
didn't have to say anything about it because we
understood each other and understood what was going on.

"Did you see Samantha?" asked Paul.

"No, no I didn't. Is she here?"

"Yeah, I just saw her. She was on her way out. You should talk to her. She would be happy to see you here."

"Yeah I think I will. Which way was she headed?"

He pointed behind us and squinted his eyes.

"Somewhere in that direction," he said.

I gave him another hug and took off in search of Sam. I got this feeling, this sense of enlightenment. *If there was something to be said, then it must be said now*, I repeated to myself. I weaved through the crowd, but to my luck, I didn't find her. I looked everywhere. I even went out back. I felt alone, perhaps more alone than ever. It was as if I was the only person in the room and the walls, again, were moving closer together. The lack of *her* hurt. This time, it was worse than any other time. I felt like a child who waited to get something, only to find out he was getting nothing. It felt as if the world was playing a cruel joke on me and everyone was in on it except me. It sliced through me and the pain was incredible. It was as if all the knives that had ever been stuck in my back were pulled out, only to be shoved back in--harder and deeper. If there was such a thing as bad luck, then this was it.

This was everything no person alive should be going through, especially alone, and even more during a viewing. Sometimes hell did exist on earth and sometimes no one could save you, not even yourself.

5

The night comforted me. I couldn't go home. I couldn't drive. Shaken, I decided to go to a lounge Samantha and I used to go to. It wasn't too far from the viewing. I needed a drink. I needed to blow off some steam. I knew I would be okay, but moments like these made me feel like hiding from the world. I had held on to this for too long. I was a fool to think that somehow, tonight would be different from all those other nights I'd spent trying to make sense of this pain she had left inside of me. I wasn't afraid to admit, I missed her, and I wasn't afraid to even say that maybe all of this was my fault, that maybe I should have tried a little harder.

I asked for a whiskey, a double. I took it down as if it was the air I needed to breathe to live. I took another double and they just kept coming in and in and I kept drinking them. Before I knew it, I was dizzy. The bill was higher than I expected. I paid $174.39 and it was money I shouldn't be spending but I had no choice. Tonight was one of those nights and I needed it, there was nothing else to do but this.

BEAUTIFUL AND DAMNED

"Are you okay to drive?" the bartender asked. Of course I said I was, even if I knew I wasn't. A lot of people are like this; no one ever wants to show a little vulnerability.

"Yeah, I'm good," I said.

The thing about being drunk, you had to be *really* drunk to not be able to drive. You had to be barely alive, almost unconscious. I mean, yeah, I had driven drunk before and I knew my limits. And, well, it's not like I had a choice. I took a deep breath and stood up from the stool. The ceiling swirled. It was as if I was stuck in a time warp, an infinite loop. By this time, I wanted to go home, crash into my dreams, and then, something crazy happened. I saw her. I saw her in all her rioting glory. She was all universes, all planets, and all moons; all skies, all lands and all oceans. I gravitated toward her like a raging comet: blindly and quickly. I stood there, about 20 feet away, as the music kept me from falling.

You know that feeling you get when someone is looking at you? For some random moment, out of all the directions I could have looked, I was suddenly eye to eye with Samantha. It was kismet as if our souls asked our bodies to turn and look. She turned her head and looked dead into my eyes. I felt as if I had died and been reborn. Maybe she died too. Maybe, in this moment, we were both dying in each other's eyes like the first time we met. We stayed looking at each other for

several seconds--seconds that felt like little
infinites and then, a taller guy, taller than me,
tapped her on the shoulder with two drinks in his
hands. Sadly, she turned away as he kissed her. He gave
her a drink and then grabbed her hand *in the way that I
used to.* She looked back at me. I stood in the same
position. I couldn't move. I went from drunk to sober
in an instant. I didn't know what to do. She looked
again and again and I just stood there as if watching
my life pass me by. You know the moment in every movie
when you feel terribly sad for the main character? This
was it. This was every sad movie I had ever seen, every
sad song I had ever heard. I was a collection of
everything that could possibly go wrong.

   Now I couldn't leave. I returned to the bar and
ordered another double. I didn't know if what I was
doing was crazy, but what I had just seen crushed me. I
mean, the entire time I thought maybe we were just on a
break, a very long break, and I wasn't dating because
of it. In fact, I wasn't even thinking about other
women, period. But seeing her with another guy, right
here in front of me, put me in a position that was hard
to ignore.

6

   She stood in line at the restroom. I knew this was
probably my only shot to talk to her.

I tapped her on the shoulder.

"Hey . . ."

"Hi"

"What happened to us, Sam?" I went straight for the kill. I didn't know how much time I had with her and I knew it was rude of me to completely disregard Stevens' death, but this was something far more important, at least to me.

"We were perfect for each other," I said quickly. "Every night I beat myself up trying to go back to see how it all fell apart. And every night, I don't find the answers. God, Sam, I just want an answer." I teared up a little. I was never good at showing emotion. I didn't even know how to cry, but I did it anyway. I didn't care and for the first time, I began to feel sorry for myself and I never saw myself doing so, but she brought something out of me. Something you only saw in empty bedrooms and lonely bathrooms. She brought out my soul and my heart. And I knew, by the way she looked at me, how I did the same to her. Only I brought out sides of her that were unclaimed and they were sides of her that only I could understand.

Sam looked me straight in the eyes. "You . . . it has always been you . . . but now it's too late. You're too late. And like you, every night for the past four months, I asked myself that same question. I asked myself what I did wrong. Where did it begin to fall apart? Why? Why? Why? I thought you had destroyed me," she said, her makeup was now smearing.

"I'm sorr--"

"Don't tell me that you're sorry," she said carefully. "I waited for you . . . and you didn't destroy me. I'm still here. I'm still laughing and dancing and getting myself back together. You didn't break me, although you might think you did. I broke myself. Most people have this terrible misunderstanding of what hurts. If I loved you, it's because I fell into it, not because you pushed me off the edge. I jumped. I fell. I got hurt. Me. Me. Me. And right now, it's all about me, and I'm trying--trying very hard to forget you. There are times when I feel like I can't forgive you or myself. I'm just so devastated!" She looked away, as did I. There were no other words.

"Look, I know I messed up," I admitted. "I messed up in the worse way possible, but I didn't know what to do. I didn't know how to handle it, how to call you, how to see you. You think I didn't want to go to your house and knock at your door?"

"Then why didn't you? Why couldn't you?"

"I don't know . . . I don't know why I didn't. Maybe I was afraid. Afraid of you rejecting me, of you telling me you had moved on. And now, I can clearly see you *have* moved on and like you, this hurts. Seeing you hurts; seeing you with that guy hurts, and right now, I don't know what to think or feel or do. I just want to go away, far away, far from you, the world, and everything I know," I said.

Tears streamed down her cheeks. My eyes got watery. The embarrassment and humiliation turned into anger and determination, but none of that really mattered. None of it gave me the answers I was looking for.

"I'm going to go," I said. "This has obviously been a mistake. I'm sorry for your cousin and I'm sorry to have interrupted you. I have to go."

I ran out as fast as I could. I hopped in my car and drove off. There was nothing for me there. She had become a graveyard-a graveyard where I didn't want to stand alone.

I was on the highway and began to feel the alcohol again. Everything began spinning and then a loud sound came from every direction. I couldn't move. I thought, perhaps this was all a bad dream and maybe it was. I had gone through so much in the last 24 hours that it was probably time for me to wake up, that is, if this was a dream.

7

I couldn't hear anything. I couldn't feel anything. My body was numb. I felt like I was watching myself lying on the pavement. The pavement was cold and wet. I could hear familiar sounds, but right now I couldn't make out any of it. I couldn't remember much. Actually, I couldn't remember anything at all. Not my name or where I came from. I couldn't remember what I was doing right before this happened or how I got there. I just felt lost and in a moment everything I thought I knew was everything that was setting me further apart from all I had been chasing for so long.

They say that life has a funny way of teaching you things. Well, I must say that whoever *they* are, they're right. Because one moment, I was driving, and then the next I was here. Confused. In an unfamiliar place-- somewhere between where I am and where I should be. I just couldn't figure out what it all meant.

The ground felt wet and cold. I felt things, things I shouldn't be feeling, things that were out of my reach. I was disoriented. I felt like I was watching myself die, to be born, then to watch myself die again and again. All my days, all my hours, and all my seconds felt still.

BEAUTIFUL AND DAMNED

Why was I lying on the ground? How strange but then again, everything that was going on was strange, at least to me.

Light rain began to fall. *Was the sky crying? Did I do something wrong?* I still couldn't make sense of anything. *How long had I been lying there?* Everything was in slow motion, distorted. I felt like I was in a movie and this was probably the bad part. I couldn't move and my body felt heavy. Hell, even my thoughts felt heavy.

The rain drops fell all onto my face and body. Everything was getting closer. Everything seemed to be closing down and my thoughts--I couldn't control them. The seconds felt like hours. And the hours felt like days and the days felt like years. And then, I remembered who I was and about how long it had been since I'd seen *you* happy. How long it had been since I'd seen *your* smile. I couldn't remember much, but the only thing that appeared in my mind was *you*.

I heard sirens. I knew something had happened, I just couldn't see and nothing was making any sense . . . but *you* . . . *you* made sense, all of you. A picture of you, your face, the shape of your hair and your nose, all of you made sense. The way your eyes moved when you were looking at the world and the way you laughed when you would catch me staring. It was you. The last image you left behind flickered through my skull like a lit match blinking on the end of the world.

Did I just crash? Was I going to die? Was I just in a bar? Am I hurt? Why can't I move? Why can't I remember how I got here? My mind was racing, but again, all I could think of was you. I just couldn't forget you.

I was beginning to lose consciousness. Everything looked blurry. I tilted my face slightly toward the left and this never-ending darkness came over me. I was consumed and before I knew it, the lights went out and I became one with the bitter nothingness of the world.

8

By the time I awoke, the doctor said three weeks had passed. I was in a near fatal car accident and intoxicated when it happened. He said it was a miracle that I was alive. I had gone through several blood transfusions and two surgeries--both of my legs were amputated. He asked me about my family, because sadly, there was no one in the room with me. No one was there to actually claim me. He did say there was a girl. And he mentioned how she had been here since I got in. He explained several different things and then he told me to get some rest. I couldn't really talk. My body was undergoing so much pain. I had to close my eyes for a second and try to forget the internal chaos.

BEAUTIFUL AND DAMNED

I barely had my eyes open and she was there.
Samantha was holding my hand tightly. I couldn't talk;
I couldn't move my jaw. She looked at me and cried and
she cried profusely.

"I love you so much, so much," she said.

A tear fell from my left eye.

"I . . . lo . . . you . . ." I said, struggling to
say these three little words, these three little words
that I almost died for, these three little words,
powerful enough to change my world in an instant.

[*I love you.* The only words worth anything in this
world, the reason we all want to live, to say these
words and to receive them back just as equally. She
loved me and I loved her and I always loved her. I
would have gone through this ordeal again and again and
again . . . to wake up with her by my side and hear her
say those three little words.]

SUNFLOWER

1

I still remember the day I ran away. I didn't look back because I let my anger get in the way. I built walls from the heat in my eyes and the day I left, I didn't think twice about it. For many years, I blamed my family and to this day, I still blame them, all of them.

When I was growing up, I always felt different. I felt out of place, as if I was missing or as if there was something *missing* within me that wouldn't let me feel as if I was home. My brother and I never got along and I hated that. I never really had anyone to cling to, anyone to let myself go with, nor anyone to listen to all the things I had to say. I always felt like I was too much and maybe that was the problem. Maybe I loved too much and showed it too little.

It had been about four years since I spoke to any of them. There had been many times that my brother and mother had tried to reach me, but every time the phone rang, I would frown and my eyes would dive deep into the back of my head. I would get angry and I never understood why I couldn't pick up the phone. I would let it ring until it went to voicemail. I guess a part of me was still running and it bothered me and they bothered me, everything bothered me. I didn't know why I felt this way but I do recall how growing up wasn't easy. It was hard and no child growing up should ever feel the things I had felt.

I now lived alone and loved it, but there was always something eerie about living alone, something that would haunt me, something terrifying that took me many years to get used to. For every time I came home, the apartment felt lonely and empty. I could no longer hear my mother's sweet voice in the backdrop and the harmonious tone of my brothers bickering throughout my parent's home. There were still a few little things I missed, a few little things I couldn't run away from. No matter how much I detached myself from them, there was always something missing. It was something that made wherever I went feel like everything else *but* home.

It was 8:31 a.m. and I was getting ready for work. I worked as a traditional artist for a local newspaper. I was always fond of art; that was my thing. Whenever I felt out of place, I would create a world where I felt most comfortable in. Imagine if it all could be that simple. *How different would my life be if I embraced all of my colors and broke down all of my barriers?* There are no rules in art and maybe that's why I'd feel

as if it was an escape every time I grabbed a pencil
and paper. It was the perfect marriage. The
relationship between the pencil and the paper was
perfection, holy.

The phone rang. I did not pick it up because I was
getting ready to go to work. I grabbed my new pallet,
one I just bought last night. It was a new set of
watercolors. I also bought a few granite pencils to
try. I put them all inside my backpack. The phone rang
again. I ignored it, as I thought about what I was
going to take for a snack. I didn't think twice about
who was calling me. I thought if it was that important,
then whoever was calling me would leave a voice
message.

I opened my refrigerator and looked around with my
tired eyes. I grabbed a bottle of apple juice and a bag
of potato chips. I put them inside of my book-bag. I
walked to the bathroom and looked in the mirror. The
phone rang a third time. I walked over to the counter
where my phone was charging and I saw two missed calls
from my brother and one from my father. I didn't think
anything about it. All I did was stare at my phone with
a blank face, letting the seconds pass. The call went
directly to voicemail. I thought about calling them
back, but I would always think about calling them
back but never did. I was just too angry to do so. I
put my phone on silent, grabbed my backpack, and turned
off the lights. As I waited for the elevator, a shot of
nervous energy ricocheted through me. I wondered why

they were calling me. I would never return their phone calls. I just wanted to forget, forget it all. Forget where I came from and all the people I knew.

I hated my memories because my family wasn't in them. I always felt like we were not a real family. My father believed that if he provided for us all, that was enough. Not once did he ask me about myself, not once did he ask me what I loved or what I was going through while I was growing up. Because of it, I always felt a little cold, distant--and with my brother, I was no different. He would bully me to make his friends laugh and I dreaded that. I dreaded both of them, my father and my brother. My mother was the only one kind of close to me, but barely. The only reason I was angry with her was because of that day and what had happened. I could never forgive her and perhaps, in some sense, I was angry with her the most because of it.

I got into my car and turned on the engine. I let it warm up. It was cold--far colder than any of the days this week, but the day was still beautiful and I could feel there was something in the air. Maybe today was the day for something beautiful to happen.

2

When I got to work, I was late. The traffic was like a broken glass squeezed tightly into a jar thrown into the ocean and it was drifting slowly.

It had taken me nearly 45 minutes to get there. My boss was in her office and my co-workers were all arriving so I didn't feel as if I was too late. I quietly snuck behind my desk and began to place my new art pigments into my drawers. I lit my desk lamp and turned on my computer. I had skipped breakfast so I opened the chips, walked back to my desk, and checked my email to see what was pending. I would create illustrations for the editorial team. My job would consist of that and that alone.

Time passed and it was nearly time to go home. I had completely forgotten about my phone. I usually kept it charging on top of my computer, but I guess I was so caught up with my work that I just forgot to place it there. That would happen to me often. Sometimes I would get so distracted by my job that I would forget almost everything. I looked at my phone and it had collected 17 more missed calls from my brother. That was rather unusual, considering for the past four years, he would only call once every three to four weeks. For a minute, I thought about calling, but I quickly changed my mind. I couldn't stomach the thought of it. I couldn't let myself be broken down. I had created these walls, these barriers, and there was nothing in the world that could break them other than me. I turned off my computer, washed my paint brushes, cleaned up my work space and said bye to almost all of my co-workers.

"See you tomorrow, goodnight." I waved my hand as I exited through the back door.

BEAUTIFUL AND DAMNED

I looked at my phone again and I noticed there were
a few voicemails too. I tried not to think too much of
it. It was out of the ordinary. Maybe they had
something to say or maybe it was just one of those
days. I was surprised my mother hadn't called, but none
of that mattered. As I drove home, I thought about it
on and off, and then it began gnawing at me. I wanted
not to care but something inside of me kept nagging--
telling me to call him back, but then, I kept reminding
myself of that day and why I had left to begin with.

When I got home, I opened the door, turned on the
lights, and just stood there. I reached for my phone
and looked at the missed calls and voicemail
notifications. I stood there, alone. I stood there as
if I was the last person on the planet and for a
second, I felt myself sink into myself. I didn't want
to pick up the calls but something inside me begged me
to call them back. I reached over my screen, cleared
out the history, and deleted the voicemails. Rage and
hurt flew through me. I couldn't straighten myself out.
I got the feeling that I didn't know how to live, a
sense of wanting to get up and walk away. For a moment,
I actually felt like what I was doing was wrong.

My phone vibrated. It was my brother again, I stood
there, numb and heavy. My thumb hovered over the answer
button until the ringing stopped. In some way, well, in
a lot of ways, ignoring my brother kind of hurt me. It
stung a little and it felt like tiny needles were
puncturing my hands. I walked to the bathroom, twisted

the sink faucet, and let the water flow out. I bent
down, letting the water pour over my head. I put my
hands over my eyes and pressed tightly. I took a deep
breath and then something happened. Something I had not
done in years. I cried. I yelled. I fell to the ground.
I flinched and trembled. My soul ached. My heart
pounded as if the weight of the sun existed within it.
Hot tears fell down my face and my nose clogged. I felt
like I had gone mad for a few moments as I wiped the
tears and just sat there on the bathroom floor. Why did
I feel this way? Why couldn't I fix this? I watched
myself die a little every day. And I watched myself be
born, too. Day in and day out, I sought death and life
and the more I tried to forget my family, the more I
would remember them. The more I tried to push them
away, the closer they all would appear in my heart.

My body felt as if it was spinning and my mind was
flat. Staring at the white ceiling calmed me. It just
made sense. No markings, no rough edges, and no cracks.
A lot less like people and more like something simple.
I felt normal at the moment and for the first time, in
a long time, I felt at home. Everything seemed
welcoming and being inside a small, white room made me
feel less alone.

By the time evening came I felt normal. I had
completely gotten over it and I was now lying in my
bed. There was something about crying, something sacred
that helped you in such a way that nothing else could.
It cleansed the stains on your soul; it pulled you up

from drowning; it rescued you. It was a beautiful thing
and I appreciated it. In a way, I admired those who
pushed me enough to cry. That's how I knew how much I
cared, no matter how much I told myself I didn't. If I
cried, it was only because I cared. All tears came from
the soul and anything that came from the soul was real.
And I knew deep down inside, somewhere in the darkness
of it all, I did care, but not enough to change all the
things that would prevent me from finding more than
just a little peace.

3

A sound coming from outside woke me in the middle of
the night. I always had trouble sleeping; anything
would wake me. My phone blinked red. I had a new voice
message. It was 3:39 a.m. and I was still wondering why
my brother kept calling. I knew it was wrong not to
return the call and I felt terrible about it. I
couldn't explain why I did that; there was just
something about him and the rest of my family that made
me feel uncomfortable. And the more I thought about why
I left, the more I hated everything. I stared at the
blinking light and decided to listen to one voicemail.

"Noah, I've been calling you all day. It's about
mom; she's not doing so well. Please call back." His
voice cracked.

I could almost feel him. I could hear this untold shade of black coming from his words like a tidal wave swallowing our planet whole. His breath faded away, echoing into the nothingness of nothing. I replayed the message several times.

Noah, I have been calling you all day. It's about mom; she's not doing so well. Please call back." His voice echoed, far away and empty, leaving and then returning.

Each time I replayed the message, a chill raced down my spine. A ghostly sensation--as if death touched every hair on my body. Then it hit me, shaking my world--my brother's voice, one that I had not heard in four years, one I had tried too hard to forget. I played the message again.

Noah, I have been calling you all day. It's about mom; she's not doing so well. Please call back. His voice was broken then whole then lost and then found.

My hands clenched and my jaw tightened. I thought about how I had been so selfish. I had detached myself from my family because of my insecurities. I never connected with anyone, but maybe it was because I shut everyone out--the moment I felt threatened. I didn't know who I was and all the things I used to help me discover myself were the same things that confused me. *What was I doing?* Why did those close to me have to pay

233

the price? I didn't know myself anymore. I'd let my anger get the best of me.

As I listened to the message, I thought about calling him back, but it was late. I figured that I'd push myself to call him in the morning, but I knew the news that our mother was not well would prevent me from going back to sleep so I grabbed my phone and without another thought, called him.

The phone rang twice. My brother picked up, his voice was weak and full of slumber.

"Hey."

A voice I hadn't heard in years. It took me back to the deepest chambers of my memory. I couldn't recall why, but I kind of missed him. I had been so detached from him and everyone else and it was kind of nice to hear someone familiar; despite all the problems.

"Noah, are you there?"

I froze for a few seconds. All he could hear was my breath--in and out like waves in a storm, in short intervals. Everything seemed loud, my heartbeat, my breathing, and even my own thoughts. The voice message had caught me completely off guard. It was hard for me to do this. It took a lot of guts. I had to stomach everything and put it all behind me. I knew there was a time and place for everything and just right now, in

this very moment, nothing mattered other than the fact
that there was something wrong with our mother. I had
to be brave. I knew I had it in me and then, in a split
second, I answered.

"Yeah, I'm here. I got your message. I . . . I just
haven't had a chance to get back to you. What exactly
is going on?"

"You have been gone for too long, my brother. It's
nice to hear you again," he said.

I could hear the frustration in his voice. It
trembled not in fear but rather in anger. It stung.

"Yeah, I know . . ."

"Mom is sick," he said as he cleared his throat.
"Mom has not been doing well for the last couple of
months," he continued. "We've been trying to reach out
to you to tell you. She needs you. *We* need you."

"What's wrong with her?"

"She's in a coma, Noah. She's in Metro Hospital.
They admitted her yesterday morning and it doesn't look
good."

"Are you there now?"

"No, visiting hours are from 6 to 11. Dad is with her."

"I'll be there tomorrow."

"Please come, Noah."

"Okay."

"Okay, see you then."

Some things never change--like that feeling you get when you haven't seen or heard about someone for some time. That feeling of the two people starting right where they left off. And then, some things do change, like two people growing further apart from each other, but also remembering the little things, the little similarities that could string them back together as if nothing ever happened or as if nothing ever caused them to drift apart. And the worst part was, I wasn't even sure to which I belonged.

4

The next day, I woke up exhausted. I had stayed up late and fallen asleep in my chair. I picked up my phone to send a text message to my boss:

"I can't make it today. I haven't been able to sleep. I spoke to my brother last night and my mother

is very ill. I'm going to see what's going on today.
Let me know if there's an emergency. Also, tell Joey to
take care of project 4892. The files are located in the
z-drive in a folder named 'crest art'. Thank you. We'll
talk soon."

I rarely missed work and when I did, I'd always
have a pile of pending projects waiting for me the next
day. One day out could ruin my week and I hated that. I
stayed in my bed for a few minutes. The room was chilly
as if winter had snuck in and stayed a while longer.

"Is everything okay?" my boss texted back.

I wrote back:

"I don't really know. I'm waiting to see what's
going on. She's in the hospital. It doesn't look too
good. I haven't been able to rest. I'm taken aback by
all of it. It feels surreal, not really registering
right now."

"Okay, take care of that. Let me know if you are
coming tomorrow," he texted.

"Okay." I wrote and sent the message back.

I moved to my bed. Alone in my room, I began to have
flashbacks of my childhood. I closed my eyes and
searched the drawers of my memory. I carefully picked
old moments and instantly, I fell into my mind like

falling into a black hole. I saw no one but my brother and I. We were walking home from high school.

"What's going on with you lately? You've been acting weird," my brother had asked while we crossed the street. I looked down at the sidewalk. I hated those little moments. The moments when my brother would pretend to be a brother because I wasn't talking on the way home.

"You could tell me. I won't tell mom and pop," he insisted.

"The thing is, I don't feel like talking."

He stopped in front of me and smiled. It was a hot day. I remember this because sweat dripped from his face.

"Noah, you're my brother. Tell me what's wrong," his voice was calm and mellow. "You think I can't tell if something is wrong with you? Something is bothering you today." His eyebrows rose and his cheeks swelled. I stood silently.

"You're not going to tell me?" he sputtered. He stood motionless for a few seconds and then shoved me.

"You're an asshole, Noah."

Actually, it was the other way around. Or maybe it *was* me. Maybe I was an asshole and I was too much of an asshole to even see that I was an asshole. But I was angry with him because he and his friends always humiliated me in front of my class and it was brutal. I hated my brother because of that. And that was one of the many reasons why I had left, why I had detached myself from him. It was a collection of these horrible memories that led me to leave. My brother and I could never get along. Even if he tried to be a good brother; within the next two minutes we would be in different rooms, in different worlds. There was never a balance between us. If I wanted something, it was because I knew I couldn't have it, and when he had something, he acted as if he didn't need it. I guess in a strange way, we were the same. We were never happy with one another because we always expected more.

5

I began to stress knowing that I would see my father, let alone my brother. I knew it was bound to happen, eventually, I just didn't think it would be under these circumstances. I hated these predicaments. I would avoid them at all cost, no matter what. I hated confrontation or maybe it was because I just didn't care enough. They had destroyed everything I was--a loving, caring person. I was hardened now and the world was even harder, but this was how it operated. This was how change happened. And once again, I had been thrown into the fire; to walk out of it reborn and full of its burning glory.

I sent my brother a text to get directions to the hospital. There was something about hospitals, something about walking down the hallways and passing by open rooms. You were able to see the patients lying down, surrounded by their families, and I wasn't sure if that was a beautiful thing or a sad, terrible thing. And no one thinks of this until they are put into this type of situation, but hospitals are like museums. They display your life's work, exhibit your show for a few moments, and then, by the time you got there, its curtains were folding, and they were closing the exhibition. In a way, people were like art. Their show could be over and if you weren't paying close attention, you'd miss it. You might even completely miss the person you went to see or why you were even there to begin with. But that's life. It is one grand show and if you're lucky, you'll go out with a bang and the world will remember you for all the colors you left behind in the sky.

When it was time to go to the hospital, my body felt as if I were already there and had already lived through whatever it was I would soon encounter. I knew it was bad. If my brother didn't sound how I remembered him, then it was bad. If he called me 19 times, then it was bad, and if he picked up my phone call within two rings in the middle of the night, then yes, it was bad. I was already expecting the worse and I didn't know how

I felt about it. It had been so long. My family was just a small group of people I used to know. But deep down inside, I knew something was prepared to bloom out of me, to bloom out of what was currently going on, like that day, the day that changed everything, the day that pushed me toward the edge of the world. If my mother was bound to die then to be honest, I didn't know how I felt about it. Or maybe I just didn't know myself enough to know what I was supposed to feel. I had never lost anyone and wasn't ready to, but this was the way things were and sometimes, that's how it was meant to be. Something's should never be tampered with. Death was the easy part; the hard part was living and knowing you could have had been better. Knowing you could have been closer and knowing how running away was never the answer, to explain the emptiness I created while I was trying to make sense of myself.

I barreled toward a wall. I knew something big was about to happen. I could feel it breathing beneath my battered bones.

There were 15 minutes left until visiting hours began. I headed to the hospital feeling as if my body and my mind were slowly floating apart. I'd get this sensation when I didn't know what else to feel. It was when your mind would leave your body because it didn't know what else to do. Similar to the feeling I got when I left my family. I just picked up my things and walked off. I didn't leave a note, I didn't say goodbye, and I didn't look back. Maybe I just didn't care. All I left

behind was my heart and I knew to them, it meant
nothing because that's how I felt my entire life. And
all I could think about was--how the older I got, the
more people would leave or disappear. That's just how
life worked sometimes. Like one day you will be missing
the company of someone and then the next day you will
remember a little less that they are gone. And it
didn't make me a bad person not to care and to move on
because like I said: that's life and sometimes that's
just how people are.

I got to Metro Hospital, pulled in, and looked for
parking. You would have thought this was an amusement
park-the place was packed. Finally, I found a parking
space and sat there for a few minutes. I thought about
everything again. I thought about how distant we had
all become. I was about to reunite with a group of
people I was supposed to call my family. I didn't want
to go through with it, but it was mother. I knew I
would regret it if I didn't come to see what was going
on. Little did I know what she was going through, but I
just had to do it, no questions asked.

I searched for building 4. The hospital was like a
maze--tall towers and narrow walkways. I found the
building and went directly to the front reception. The
lady at the desk had dark freckles and light skin. Her
hair was picked up in a bun. She typed frantically. As
she struck the keyboard with her fingers, each pound
sounded like machine guns firing at the faces of those

sitting in the lobby but nonetheless it was quiet, perhaps a little too quiet.

"Good afternoon," I said with my hands in my pocket.

"How may I help you, young man?"

"I'm here for Rosa Mason. She was admitted yesterday." My voice was light and shy like a feather being thrown through a window.

"Mason . . . Mason . . . let me see . . ." She tapped on her keyboard; her eyes glanced rapidly across the screen. Up and down, side to side. She scrolled through the screen and then squinted as if she was watching through the crack of a closet.

"Here she is, yes, room 513. May I see your ID, young man?"

I pulled my wallet from my back pocket, opened it, and handed her my driver's license.

"Okay, let me get this done for you." She took the ID and scanned it. Soon after, she gave me a visitor sticker with my face on it.

"Thank you," I said as I put the sticker on my shirt.

"Visiting hours end at 11 p.m."

"Okay, thank you," I said as I walked toward the elevator. What was unusual was that the elevator had a couch in it; a very awkward place to have a couch. I guess they wanted to make the hospital feel homey because, in a way, it did. In an awful way it did. I felt calm and the stiffness from hearing the news about my mother loosened up a bit. I got in and hit 5. The button shined. It had a nice appeal to it, similar to the moon the other night. As I went up to the 5th floor, time suddenly slowed, and my heart began to pound. I went numb; my entire body felt as if it had been in a bucket filled with ice. Little chills declared war on my skin. As the elevator ascended, my stomach dropped and everything that was going on nauseated me.

Things seemed to be careening toward an unknown. Whatever the news was, I knew I wasn't ready for it. No one ever is. That's just not the way things work. You don't arrive to life with a disaster manual. These kinds of things just happened. And when they did, they came hard, like an earthquake digesting an entire city. One minute, you're laughing, and then the next you're sobbing. And the hard part was to pretend things like this didn't happen and living your life as if everything was perfect. But the worst part of it all was this: when it did happen--and it eventually will-- you can't pretend things would be okay from here on out. That's not the way life worked. Life would give you something beautiful and once it knew you needed it, then, that's when it happens. Life's a bitch like that.

Sometimes, in any given moment, it could take everything that meant the world to you, take it away forever, and leave you with nothing.

The elevator dinged, its doors opened slowly as if it knew I was bound to walk into terrible news. I felt like I was in the middle of the ocean. I took my first step off the elevator and almost lost my balance. This floor was quiet; all I could hear was the light chatter coming from the far rooms.

My chest felt like a chain of bombs were being dropped from war planes. I looked to my left and saw room 514 and looked to my right and saw room 516. I kept walking; it was confusing. I wasn't sure if the room numbers were going up or down, but hospitals were like that; they confused the hell out of people. I looked back and there was room 513. Its door was slightly open; I knew my father was in there because my brother said he planned to stay with mother overnight.

As if I was sneaking into my own room, I slowly opened the door. No one was there. No father, no brother, no doctor and no nurse; only mother and she was asleep. Suddenly, I froze. Mom looked different; she looked old and beaten by time. It had been four years since I last saw her. Her light scent bloomed; it smelled like summer and rain all together. She was asleep and I walked in without a sound. Something stirred inside of me and it felt like broken glass being crushed from within. It felt like something

245

wanted to surface. It pulsated. I didn't like this feeling, not one bit. I just stood there trying to make sense of what was going on. The room was dark with a ray of sunlight coming through the slight space between the curtains. It had one small table in the center and two chairs near the curtains. The heart monitor beeped like a skipping record. Each beep echoed like thunder swirling through the empty space of time. Each beep disappeared into the walls of the room.

I sat down; my eyes fixated on my mother. I couldn't blink. I brought the chair closer to her and held her hand. It felt warm, like I'd never left her side. It was the two of us, alone, trying to find meaning in this life and the next. And then something happened, something that was beyond me. I couldn't breathe and my soul seemed to rumble inside of me. I grabbed my mother's hand and held it toward my face. I began to think of how terrible I had been. I had pushed her away. Everyone that had ever tried to get close to me, I had pushed away. No wonder I was alone. It was because of me. And I had thought that the world was at fault and blamed it for all of my failures. I had been pointing my finger at the people who cared about me the most but it was all my doing. I cried until it turned into sobs. I couldn't control myself. It all came out; everything I had been storing inside for so long just poured out like water spilling from a tipped glass. I felt awful, my entire being was filled with storms and they were the kind of storms that would knock the wind out you.

"Why do you cry, boy?"

For a second, I thought I was dreaming. *Had I just heard my mother's voice?*

"What troubles you, Noah?" Her voice was soft like water and her tone low. It was loud enough for me to hear but low enough for the rest of the world to ignore.

"You know when you cry, you still have the same face you used to make when you used to cry in my arms as a child." She smiled as she turned her head towards me.

That's the thing about mothers. You could be an old man and they would still see you as a child, no matter what. I wiped my face and smiled back. She had an oxygen support mask on. Her eyes spoke to me; they always did, and then, with a faraway stare, she looked at me and smiled some more. I didn't know what to say. I was in tears and I slightly laughed. I guess in a way she knew what I wanted to say and I didn't have to explain myself. She just understood how awful I had been and in some sense, she had forgiven me. We smiled at each other a little more and the tears kept falling from my eyes.

"Mom . . . I know I've been--"

"I know baby. I know." She squeezed my hand and kept looking into my eyes. A tear fell from her face. I was

ashamed, embarrassed, but there was nowhere to hide.
After all, I had been running for four years. There
comes a time when we all must stop running and face our
fears no matter what the outcome is.

"Do you remember the time we went to the sunflower
garden? When your father and I were young and you and
your brother were little children?"

"Yes I do, of course, I do."

"Those were the best times of my life. Those
sunflowers were nearly 6 feet tall and I felt like I
was standing in a golden ocean. I could have spent
hours getting lost in the yellow waves. I miss how the
wind hit my face and tangled my hair. I wish I could go
back there, Noah, I felt free. Would you take me there
when I get out? I would like that, my son." She
struggled to whisper. Her voice was musky and it would
crack with every word she softly muttered.

"Yes, we can go as soon as you get better, I
promise," I said as my heart broke a little more.
Seeing her in this state was hard. She was fragile and
I, too, was fragile. We were both broken, but there was
a difference, my mother would take her pieces and make
them beautiful. While I, on the other hand, never knew
what to do with my brokenness. I would just run and
hide with it.

My soul shattered while she said these things. It hurt and when anything hurts it leaves a mark, a mark that would forever stain the chambers in my heart. I wanted to tell her how much I loved her, but I couldn't. I don't know why I couldn't. Maybe now wasn't the time for this. Maybe right now I just wanted her to get better. I wanted to try to rebuild anything that I might have destroyed with her and with my father and brother. We can't live our lives in regret and maybe now was the *right* time for change.

6

"Mom?"

"Yes, dear."

"What happened to me? Why am I this way?"

"What way, baby?"

"Why do I act the way I act? Like, why am I so self-conscious? Why do I run away the moment I feel like someone is getting close to me? Or why am I me? Sometimes I don't like myself for how I feel. I don't like people and I don't like crowds. I like being alone and in a strange way; I believe all of that has to do with all of you--you, Father and Brother. What I am trying to say is why didn't you guys stop me? Keep me from leaving?" My eyes began to tear again.

"You mean *that* day?"

"Yes, that day. Why didn't you tell me to stay? Why did you let me go?"

She raised her left hand and gently touched my right cheek. "Because sometimes you have to learn how to let go, let all the things you are seeking find you. Even if that means letting go of all the things you love." She smiled as her hand drifted from my face.

And right before I was going to reply back, my father and my brother walked in. They each held a cup of coffee. My father, a difficult man, was quiet and to himself. He didn't say much and most of the time, when I was growing up, he was never around. But I got used to that and I always thought maybe he was the reason I was who I was. We had a lot of similarities. For one, I didn't say much and when I did, it was because I was angry. That was probably the one good thing about being angry--the truth always seemed to come out. We were both impatient and we would only play by our own rules. If it didn't go as we planned, then we didn't want anything to do with it. We were both stubborn and to us, everyone and everything was always wrong.

Yeah, there were a lot of similarities between the two of us and sometimes when I looked at him, I felt like I was looking at a reflection of myself. There were times when he was gentle and soft and he showed a little of what he had inside. I, too, was this way. And

it was always either/or, for the both of us. If ever we
chose to let someone in, someone into our hearts, then
we would show them a different kind of warmth. The kind
of warmth people could live off and it was the kind of
warmth that made people stay. And I liked that
similarity. It was just hard to find the right person
to show it to. But that's what made us so damn special.

I got up and my brother came to give me a hug. He
looked different. His hair was thick and long. He had
braces on his teeth, but something was the same about
him. He had the same little freckles and the same
little smile. He wore black sunglasses, a tank top,
ripped jeans and old sandals. His cologne had a
distinct scent that reminded me of when we were young.
He wasn't the same, but he was. You know, when you
haven't seen someone for years and the moment you see
them, you realize how much they have changed. He gave
me another hug and asked me how long I had been waiting
here.

"A few minutes. About 15," I replied.

My father grunted and took a sip from his coffee. He
always had a problem being sensitive, especially in our
current situation. Maybe he wanted to be strong and I
would have thought how maybe he would have been more
approachable.

"How are you, Boy?" he asked as he sat down next to
me. He put his hand over mother's forehead; she was

sound asleep. I knew she was fragile and needed her
rest, so I didn't think much of it.

"I've been good," I replied without making eye
contact. It was uncomfortable for me to make eye
contact, especially with my father.

"Did it take you a long time to get here? Were my
directions good?" my brother asked.

"Yeah, I made it here on time."

It felt a little awkward. The energy in the room
overwhelmed me. I didn't know if I felt at home with my
father and brother or if I felt as if I was with two
strangers. My brother kept asking me general questions.
"How's work? Do you see anyone new? Tell me about your
life now?" It was hard to squeeze four years into 30
minutes. As we talked, my father kept to himself. He
didn't say a word. He just sat next to mother and
stared at her. I could see the weakness in his eyes;
they looked shaken by fear, the fear of what was bound
to come. A fear no one ever wanted to encounter.

By the time we spoke about anything else, half of
the visiting time had passed. After four years, my
brother felt like a friend, like a brother. I felt at
ease with him as if we had never lost touch. We laughed
about the times when we were kids. We had so much back
then. It almost felt like another life, like a dream,
as if none of the bad times had ever happened. Memories

are time machines; they can lift you off your feet,
spin you, and by the time you realize it, you're back
to where it all started, back to where it all made
sense.

   Our childhood was empty. I hated my brother most of
the time. But when I thought about it, it made me who I
was and I was grateful for that. When I asked him about
mother and what was wrong, he told me she had cancer--
she had been battling cancer for the last three years.
He said they tried to reach out to me, but it was very
hard considering they had no clue where I was living. I
felt bad. Actually, I felt awful. I knew the news was
bad from the start, but no one ever thinks the worse
even when it is. Mother was a cancer survivor. She had
a mastectomy about eight years ago. The doctor told
them it had returned, had spread throughout her body
within the last couple of months. She was in pain and
they had sent her to hospice. The more questions I
asked my brother, the more my father seemed annoyed,
angered and bothered. And then, my father stood up and
walked toward the door.

   "Get out!" He yelled as he opened the door, looking
straight at me.

   My brother and I stood in shock--thrown off and
confused by father's reaction.

   "Get out! You think you can just walk on in here and
pretend like you care about your mother? Where have you

been for the last four years? I watched your mother cry
herself to sleep because of you, you good-for-nothing.
Where were you? Where were you when she needed you?
Where were you when she picked up the phone, dialed
your number, and was forwarded to your answering
machine instead of talking to her beloved son? Where
were you?" he yelled.

"You were not here, Noah," he continued. "So don't
come here with all of this bullshit!"

A nurse from the floor's lobby walked in.

"Is everything okay in here?"

My father's face was red from the yelling. His blood
must have been raging. I had never seen him this angry,
at least not in a long time.

"We're fine. Noah was just leaving." He looked at
me, his broken face filled with broken tears. Tears
filled with anger and regret. He then took his hands
and wiped them on his face as if he were too
embarrassed to cry in front of his sons. I had never
seen father break. I stood up and looked at my brother
who was still in shock. He couldn't believe what was
going on. I looked at him and gave him a hug.

"I love you, my brother, you know that, right?" said
my brother.

It was hard for me to say it back. My brother and I had never said that to each other. I guess I wasn't comfortable enough to say it back. I did love him, but it was just . . . I couldn't say it back. Something wasn't right; perhaps it was the situation. My father stood by the door and so did the nurse.

"Goodbye, Pop." I looked him dead on and then my brother. I looked at my mother, my eyes began to swell, but I held it in. And then, without thinking twice, I looked down and quietly walked away.

7

Three days later my brother called me hysterical. Mother had died. At first, he wasn't making any sense. All I heard were loud mumbles, words clacking like tumbling lumber. It seared my mind, the way he spoke, and when he finally gave me the news, it pushed me back.

When we hung up, his voice kept haunting me. I wasn't used to him sounding like that. Every time you get news like this, you lose your mind a little. Like I said before, nothing can prepare you for it. No matter how many times you've experienced a death in your family, each time you get this sort of news, you die a little more until it's your turn to go and then you don't have to think about losing more people you love. And it's only in the very last second of life, that

last second when you take your last breath, when most
of us seem to discover what the meaning of all of this
was. What life meant to us. I believe in our last days,
everything you have been seeking comes to you and it
comes to you in the strangest ways, like a flash
banging in front of your face.[A meaning that is too
hard to ignore and it is up to all of us to go through
life waiting for this day to happen, the day when
everything and everyone understands why they were put
on this earth to begin with.]

I took the news very hard. It ripped me. It killed
me. The air from my lungs sucked out like vacuum and
the moment we hung up, I felt the room closing in.
Nausea over took me, I couldn't believe it. The room
felt small and then I felt small. I was alone; I had no
one to talk to and what a terrible thing it was to have
to go through it alone. Not one person to comfort your
weeping. What a terrible thing it was to feel as if a
thousand demons were laughing at you as you gasped for
air in the middle of an empty earth. What a dreadful
thing it was to have your nightmares visit you and
greet you with laughter. It was all so horrifying. My
life, my family, my friends, my job, my apartment, it
was all so depressing and nothing in this earth could
save me from myself. I wanted to do something, but I
didn't know what. All I could do was think about my
mother and the alarming coldness death had brought to
my doorstep. I stayed in my room. I watched the day
turn to night. I couldn't eat, I couldn't get up, and I
couldn't do anything. I could only think about my

mother. I sat on my bed, alone with the darkness of my
room; my soul was like a rocking chair, drifting back
and forth, back and forth. My body numb until the
darkness vanished and the light was reborn again. The
photons snuck in through the curtains and I sat there
on my bed-paralyzed like a corpse left out to dry. I
couldn't move, but my mind was wild, alive, and
restless. I watched the night return and then the
darkness came to me again. I ignored the world and
everything in it and I just sat there on my bed for
almost two days and nights.

I had not heard from my brother. I could only
imagine what he was going through--let alone my father.
Our hearts were broken and there was nothing worse than
heartbreak, especially if the one who caused it was
someone you knew you would never see again, at least
not in this lifetime. It was tragic and I couldn't come
to my senses. I did go a bit mad, I must admit. And I
couldn't forgive myself for the distance I had created
between my mother, brother, and father. I don't know if
I would ever be able to forgive myself. I felt enslaved
by it, devoured by my insecurities, and among all
things, I did this to myself as if that day I ran away
had caught up to me just to send me straight to hell.
And now I had to live with all of this. I had to live
with the burden of my choices and die with this sharp
regret deeply buried beneath my skin and emerging from
my bones. And it hurt my soul. I wanted to blame mother
for letting me go, but it was much deeper than that. I
was my own enemy and I knew from here on out, when I

257

looked at the mirror, I would be staring into the eyes of someone I used to know.

8

The next day my brother called me. Drowning in my own insecurities, I slowly turned my head and extended my arm to grab my phone as if I was reaching out for help.

"Hey, Noah, how are you holding up?" My brother's voice was sluggish and every word dragged as if he was shoving them out, forcing himself to speak.

"Mom's viewing will be tomorrow; it's at the funeral home down Bird Street and 34th avenue. It will be from 8 p.m. 'til midnight."

"Okay," I replied softly and then he hung up, just like that, and for a moment, I felt like a branch falling from a tree. Something inside me splintered. I had never been to a viewing. I wasn't even sure what I was supposed to do. I knew I had to go, but I wasn't sure what to expect. Everything felt unreal. I felt like reaching out and calling my mother. I couldn't believe all of this was happening. I was afraid of it all, afraid of seeing my mother's lifeless body. The thought of this haunted me, already. The thought of having to go through the rest of my life without my mother felt like a cold knife pushing itself inside my

chest. I waited on my bed till the next day. I barely
got up for anything. I ignored everything. I ignored my
work friends and my life. No one outside knew of such
tragic news; just my boss. I didn't want anyone to know
what I was going through. I never liked being too open
with personal issues, with family things, with things
like this, things that really mattered.

I never liked how some people were--just out to get
you, and if they saw you falling, they would pretend to
be there for you. Pretend to care, as if the problem
was their very own. No one can ever say, "I understand
what you're going through" or "I'm sorry for your loss"
because no one ever understands. We are not meant to be
understood. I would rather have someone just be here,
silent, not saying a word, then have someone try to
comfort me with bullshit. I was miserably broken, lost,
and not a soul in the world could mend me back to
whole. Not a single soul to talk to and not a single
soul to make me feel a little less cold. But that's how
people were; they were expected to be there and they
would also expect you to do the same, which is why I
was alone, and why I will always be alone. For I never
wanted someone to expect such things from me,
especially things I knew I could never fulfill.

You know, they say life works in mysterious ways--
like when you lose someone, you find someone else. But
what happens when you lose a brother? A mother? A
father? Or a child? These people can't be replaced. In
such circumstance, we tend to lose more than just

someone we love. [We tend to lose ourselves with the fear of not ever finding our way back. At least, not return the same way you were. And if you did return, of course, you wouldn't be the same. Everything would be different, every place and every face, different. Even those that were familiar would look different. You would question everything and nothing would make sense but the fact that your whole world is square even if your entire life you had been born to believe it was round.]

The next day I woke up late. I had to take some antidepressants to calm down. They made me sleep a lot, perhaps too much, but I didn't care. My world was backwards and it had changed dramatically within a few days. I was still in shock from everything.

Today was the viewing; I didn't want to think about it. My eyes felt heavy and I was still drowsy from the medication. [I was on my bed, alone and empty. And I began to think how people come and go. You know, some things were meant to vanish in an instant and then there were some that took time to dissolve. And it was the same way with people. Some of them would disappear into the air while others burned slowly out of our lives.]

[Life had a funny way of making us feel less alone, because in the end, all that remained were empty rooms. Our minds are like empty houses filled with forgotten memories, forgotten rooms. We come and then we go. We arrive to change people's lives and then, no matter what we did or who we met, we knew how it was all meant for something, something bigger than ourselves. And when we left, we took everything with us, but it was all about those moments, those precious little moments. The ones most of us would tend to ignore or forget as time goes on.]

I remembered my mother and myself in the pool. We were smiling. I was just a small boy. She would tell me to jump into the water because I was afraid to swim. I was terrified, but she made it all comforting. She would push me because she believed I was better and she believed I could. And when I finally jumped, she was right there to greet me with open arms. And I thought jumping would kill me, but I did not die, and I did not sink. She held me when I was afraid and despite the four years I was absent, I wished she was still here to tell me how everything would be okay.

There's something beautiful about mothers. And yes, you are bound to come across people who would inspire you, love you, and change you. Those are very rare people. And then, there are mothers and what they do for their children is something beyond all of us. Something that's just too exquisite to put into words. And it killed me that she was gone. What finished me off was the last four years and how I had neglected her because I just didn't feel like connecting.

BEAUTIFUL AND DAMNED

It was almost time to go. There were about 30 more
minutes until my mother's viewing. I took whatever
energy I had left in me and got up from my bed. My room
was dark. I had all the lights off and my shutters were
tightly secured so the sunlight wouldn't come in. I
walked toward the bathroom and turned on the lights. I
looked at myself for a second. I looked normal on the
outside but deep within I was a wreck. I turned the
knob and the water rippled into the tub. I stood there
as it filled. I put my left foot in the water. It was
hot, but I didn't care. I welcomed the burn even if I
didn't want to. I sunk within the tub, while the tap
was still running. I thought some more of what my
mother had just gone through. I felt it deeply. I
thought about what she said and how the sunflower
garden had made her feel free. I thought about how much
of a son of a bitch I had been to her and why I would
ignore her calls every time she tried to reach out to
me. It had been four long years, four long and
miserable years. I sunk myself deeper in the hot water.
My entire body was under and my face was like an
island. I felt like I was barely alive. It was all so
dead inside.[I felt like I had robbed myself of my
feelings and of everything I should had been feeling. I
wasn't even sure if how I felt now was how I should
have been feeling.] I closed my eyes and my mother's
face would appear then disappear and reappear and each
time with more detail. Her smile would light the
darkness--this darkness that would befriend me as I
closed my eyes. A silence crawled from beneath the
floor and consumed me, all of me. And I stayed

262

submerged in the water until I found the courage to
face the light again.

By the time I was ready, two hours had passed. There
was something about time when someone dies, something
that made time both fast and slow. It was fast when you
wanted it to be slow and slow when you wanted it just
to pass on and finish. They say time heals everything,
but honestly, I feel like time will never be on our
side. For time has only taught us regret and regret has
always been a terrible, terrible drug--a drug that we
will never be able to recover from.

I got dressed and took a deep breath. My eyes got
swollen. I tried to stay calm. I turned off the lights
and headed out the door. It slammed as it closed and
shook me terribly. I walked toward my car, started the
engine, and drove off.

9

When I arrived at the viewing, people were in line
giving their respects and saying their goodbyes. I had
to park across the street near a run-down food market.
I wasn't sure what to do. I texted my brother and told
him I was here. I felt bad enough because I was late. I
waited for him to text me back. It took nearly 10
minutes. He walked out from the main entrance and came
directly to me. An old lady came from the other

direction. She grabbed my hand and with a deep sadness she said:

"I'm sorry for your loss. I knew your mother. She was such a beautiful person. There are no words. There are no words."

Our hands slipped from each other as the old lady passed by. My brother gave me a smile. His eyes were dark. He must have had been crying all day. His nose was red, and his face looked tired. There was this nothingness emerging from him. I could tell. His eyes looked lost. Lost somewhere between what is and what was, between our childhood and this moment of pain. I felt him and I knew he, too, could feel me. We were heartbroken, and like that lady said, there were no words. He just hugged me and he hugged me even tighter. My brother had never held on to me like this before. It felt good. It felt complete and for that very moment, I felt somewhat happy and liberated from myself.

[We just hugged each other and didn't say anything. Sometimes there were no words to explain something like this; it just was and there were no words. We just held on and we didn't know how to let go.]

"We lost Mom," he whimpered with a low tone. I didn't know how to respond. It was hard for me to express myself. It was something unreal, unearthly, and dreamlike. It felt like a nightmare. A nightmare we

both would never be able to forget and it hadn't hit me
completely just yet.

"You want to say your goodbyes?" His eyes looked
red, sore and glazed. I just stood there and nodded my
head as we went inside the funeral home. I saw all
types of people. Most of them I didn't recognize. I saw
some relatives, some I hadn't seen in years. Some who
remembered me, but I couldn't remember them. I walked
down the funeral home hallway. The lighting was soft
and lightly muted. The hallway was like the hospital--
long and intimidating. My heart raced. The air seemed
too thin and I choked. I followed my brother as the
crowd got smaller and smaller. We made a left into a
yellow room. It was blanketed with the silence of
death. Some people sat in chairs while other just stood
around. And then, I saw the casket. It was covered with
lovely flowers. I leaned closer and saw my mother. My
heart sunk. My soul dropped, I couldn't pick it up, and
then it all just fell. The feeling of death came in, a
bitter gentleness, and I, once again, felt alone. She
sank to the bottom of the casket. She looked serene and
relaxed. Her face showed sincere comfort and yet she
lay there alone, alone in all her tranquil brilliance.
All life ended and began alone. And it was only the
people we met and connected with that made our lives
feel as if we were born together.

She wore red lipstick and her scent was reminiscent
of our childhood. Her arms were crossed and she looked
like she went out with a smile. Death must have had

quivered while taking my mother because she was the
kind of woman who always greeted pain with a smile. And
that alone made her dangerous. She didn't fear anything
and that's what made her who she was.

I got closer to the casket and kneeled before her. I
put my head near her arms and teared up. [I tried to
hold it in but I couldn't. You can't hold in these
types of things; they will drive you crazy and even
kill you.] I could barely breathe, but in a way, it felt
good. Liberating. It was coming out, all of it. The
last four years, all the pain I'd ever felt, all the
pain I held within, all the pain I didn't know what to
do with-it flooded around me and it came out viciously.
I stayed drowning in my guilt and that was the worst
because I knew I had to live with the knowledge that I
could have spent the last four years creating memories
with my mother. Instead, I foolishly walked backwards
and in circles. The entire time I thought what I was
doing was right, but it was wrong. I was wrong and now,
I cursed myself for leaving that day.

I felt a warm hand press against my left shoulder. I
looked up to see my father. He helped me up and hugged
me like never before. It felt like two fires colliding
into one. Two fires lighting the sky. And for a few
seconds, our differences didn't matter. We were
together and united. Then my brother came and hugged
the both of us. We clinched closely and embraced the
moment of loss as we remembered the love of a mother
and a wife.

10

My mother was cremated the next day. My father kept her in a vase decorated with little sunflowers. My brother and I stayed with father and we laughed and shared memories. Father told us stories of when he and mom had met. My father cooked for us. He said having us around made him feel like the days when we were younger, when we were a family. He said he missed us both and then, he opened up. He told us why he was so hard on us when we were kids. He didn't know what he was doing. He never had a father. His father had divorced his mother and he never even knew who his father was. He cried, telling us both how much he had failed us as a father. Being alone was a curse he was bound to have to live with, he told us. I understood him. I, too, had been feeling this way and felt like I have failed as a son and as a brother. And as my father spoke, I discovered that the distance between us was never because of the insecurities we felt, but rather the emptiness we created when we failed to make sense of ourselves.

I now understood and I understood it well. My faults came from my father, the one man I thought I never wanted to end up like. Yet, all along, I was slowly becoming just like him.

BEAUTIFUL AND DAMNED

My brother asked me to join him outside for a smoke.

"I could never understand him," my brother said as he closed the front door.

"Me neither, but in a way, I get him now," I replied as my brother dug down in his pocket and pulled out his cigarettes. He lit one up and took a toke.

"Father is a complicated man," I said. "I hated him my entire childhood. I hated him because he was never there, but now, I understand that perhaps in some sense, he probably felt the same way about his father, too."

"You know, I don't blame him. I just feel like he could have tried," my brother said, taking a hit and then looking out to the field.

"I hated you too . . . growing up," I said quickly.

"Me?" said my brother. "Why?"

"For many reasons, but that was a long time ago."

"Let me ask you, how come you never picked up the phone when I would call you?" my brother asked.

I took a deep breath and spoke from the heart.

"I don't know. I guess I felt insecure about myself. Or maybe I didn't care enough. I felt like I wanted to start over and meet new people, make new friends. I wanted to run away from you guys. I went through a lot. Most often, I felt like none of you understood me. I wasn't simple. Hmm, I guess I don't know why I hated you."

My brother tapped me on my shoulder. It was the kind of tap you would give to a friend and it felt good.

"When I went to the hospital, mother told me about the sunflower garden. Do you remember it? It was the one she and father would take us to when we were young?" I watched my brother exhale and turn toward me.

"Mother *spoke* to you?" he asked, his tone serious.

"Yeah, right before you and father came in."

"Noah, mother was in a coma. What do you mean she spoke to you? She was unconscious the whole time she was in the hospital. She passed without ever regaining consciousness."

I didn't know what to make of it. I had spoken to my mother. I wasn't crazy. I wasn't delusional. It happened. My brother had that look of disbelief in his eyes as I explained it to him in detail. We stayed outside for a few more minutes and then we both went back inside.

BEAUTIFUL AND DAMNED

We stayed all night and again, we kept talking about mother. Together we cried, we laughed, and we did what any other family would do when a loved one passed. We kept each other's spirits high, but I knew the moment I returned home, it would be different. There's a difference between going through something horrific as a family and then going through it alone. There's only so much comfort you can find from those who care about you and then when you're alone, you must find a different kind of comfort in the loneliness--in all its foulness, in the haunting silence of your own thoughts. Thoughts kill and when they do, they just keep on killing. There is no escaping that, it never ends.

By the time I had to go, I felt different inside; as if a seed had been planted. It had been so long since I felt close to my father and brother. I felt a sweet tune playing throughout my heart and like I said, I felt different, a good different. It was a seed I knew nothing of, like a new life, a new start. It was something born from something ugly. It felt real and it attracted me. Perhaps the loss of someone meant the birth of something new and maybe this was meant to happen.

The next day all I could do was think about mother. There was no other way to put it other than that. I thought about her every second. And when it was noon, I remembered what she told me the last time we had spoken and how much she loved that sunflower garden. I was hesitant at first because I wasn't even sure if that

place still existed. It had been many years since I had
even thought about that garden but now, something told
me to go. I had that gut feeling that I was meant to go
even if I didn't want to. It was the very last thing
she said to me and I promised her I would take her.

I called my father to ask him where I could find
this place. I was far too young to remember the
address. He asked me why and I told him the story.
After I explained what had happened in the hospital, I
told him I just felt like going. He gave me the
directions and I was well on my way. I drove about an
hour and a half to get to there. To my surprise, all
that was left was land, a dry, dead space with no
sunflower field. No golden ocean. Just the dark dirt
covering what was once a beautiful dream.

I parked my car in front of the entrance. A wooden
fence surrounded the dry land. On the gate, a rusted,
white sign swung in the breeze. The words 'no
trespassing' were stamped on it: sadness and regret
covered my bones. I stood there and tears fell from my
eyes. I felt like I had just lost a dream--as if I
almost had something so precious within my grasp and
now it was gone. My heart broke-shattered in so many
ways. Not just because my mother had passed away or
because I stood in front of a dead garden, but also
because I failed myself. I was out of control and that
kept killing me. I felt like I was born into this
world; in all its violent sadness and I was a victim of

its relentlessness. I felt like I had woken up beneath the cold and it was heavy, too heavy to move forward.

I felt like I was swimming in a golden ocean. I could have spent hours getting lost in the yellow waves. I miss how the wind would hit my face and tangle my hair. I wish I could go back there Noah; I really felt free.

Her voice echoed through my mind as I looked at what was left of the garden.

From out of nowhere, a gust of wind came upon me and this was no ordinary wind. It was as if the wind went right through me and it was strong enough to collapse a building but gentle enough to calm the sea. And then, the wind surrounded me, drowning me in the light scent of summer and rain. It came from every direction and I no longer felt alone. I knew I was in good company and how everything from here on out was going to be okay.

11

A few months have passed since my mother died and ever since I've felt different about everything. I formed a new relationship with my brother and father. We would get together every Sunday. Brother and I would visit my father at his home. It was always a memorable moment. I learned the value of family. I learned the

importance of seeing pass the labels society had
created and the ones we create for ourselves. Those are
barriers. I broke all the walls down and became friends
with both of them. And that seed, that little seed I'd
felt was another side of me, one I never knew I had. I
began to open up to people, to see how beautiful it was
to have friends and bonds. I began to like crowds and
socializing. I was a different man. I liked hearing
about people's lives and I had an interest in what
other people had to say. Everyone was special in their
own way and I always had something new to learn about
them.

I fell in love but not with someone or something. I
fell in love with my life. For the first time in a long
time, everything inspired me. Everything felt vivid and
real and I had a connection with it all.

And that day, the day I ran from it all, got lost in
new days, and it slowly flickered out of my memory. And
then, there were always those nights, those nights when
I would leave my friends, when I would leave my family,
and I would come home to my empty apartment. Alone. And
sometimes, I felt lost. And those were always the most
horrifying of nights, but always, always in the midst
of it all, something strange would happen, no matter
where I was . . . whether I was home or at work or with
company or not. A sudden breeze carried the scent of
summer and rain. And it would always surround me. It
would take me back to the sunflower garden. Mother's

sunflower garden and it reminded me how I was never
meant to be alone.

THE DAMNED

BE SOFT. BE FRAGILE.

THE NIGHT ESCAPE

It's been a while since
I last went out,
perhaps too long--
or long enough for me
to dream of crowds.
Sometimes you just have to
go out there and experience
life a little.
You can't always stay
in and expect to learn
something new about people
by reading books.
Human understanding
does not work that way.

You have got to feel the people,
not read about them.

I went to Wood Tavern one night
and, of course, it was a rare thing
for me to see this place so empty.

"There are too many people." I thought.
Too many faces and they are all waiting
for something, like a spaceship,
something to come out of the sky

BEAUTIFUL AND DAMNED

and tell them how beautiful they are
and they are; every single one of them.

Anyway, it felt good to be out
so I walked to the bar
and someone spilled a drink on me.
(This is how good turns bad.)

The girl turns around and says
"Sorry." then turns back around
and goes on with her night.

Now my shirt was wet, but
I, too, went on with my night.
I drank, I laughed, and I forgot
how I left.

When I got home I sat in front of the
old typewriter and wrote this here prose
you are reading right now.

I typed and thought,
I thought and typed.

And I still do not understand
humans at all, including myself.

WOMEN. WOMEN. WOMEN.

Her hair was always covered with flowers
and I swear you could almost see
the sun rise from the corner of her eyes.

Her eyes like two moons crowding the sky.

I look away; something far out there distracts me,
and then, I look at her again
and I remember what it felt like
when I saw the ocean for the first time.

She takes me away, far away,
and maybe even far enough.

I could go on about her forever.

If there's a paradise, then it exists inside
other people, and I swear, everyone
deserves at least one.

Mine was five foot six
with long hair and a nice smile.

DO THINGS ALONE

I feel the same way.
You feel the same way.
Everyone feels the same way.
And we do not know
how to tell each other.
We just want a way
out of our own inhumanity,
out of our own skin.
The world has made us believe
how we are not beautiful,
how we are not capable
of becoming art.

But I see you walking.

I see the paint falling off
your shoes as if I see Van Gogh,
Michelangelo, and Picasso
were pouring out of the way
you move.
You are beautiful,
and the world wants to
mutilate your story.
It wants to erase the words
so we all think the same.

So we all think less.

I need you to know you are
more. You have to see it,
open your eyes.

You are different.

You are beautiful,

but we don't feel that way
about ourselves.

BETWEEN US

You cannot be different
because if you are different
then all the people will follow you,
and be different like you
and that will make all of us
the same.
You cannot be a writer,
then everyone wants to be
a writer.
You cannot be an athlete,
a musician, a painter
because then everyone wants to
do those things, and your
specialty becomes a small
piece of the normal, a normal
that is a piece of an even bigger
piece of an even bigger piece
of the normal.

"Well, that makes life
hard to look forward to."

Of course, it does.
There is nothing much
to look forward to.

ROBERT M. DRAKE

No originality. No humanity.
No love. No creation.

All I see are bodies pilling
up everywhere I go.
Pilling up in the stores,
in the bars, and in the street.

It's hard to be more.
Everything is a stain of
everything else.

Therefore, I am a version
of someone else,
of something else.

And that makes life hard to live.
It makes it impossible
to run away from.

I am you and you are me

and together we make *everyone*.

THEY ARE DANGEROUS

There are things a woman can do to a man without the use of words.

I went to Kitchen & Bar, a local lounge here in Wynwood, Miami. The night was as expected: slow and quiet. Not many people stay up after 1 in the morning on a weekday.

A beautiful woman entered the room and she lit up like Las Vegas.
A man watched her, approached her and bought her a drink. She asked for a dirty martini, which I hate.

They stayed talking for a few and from what I remember he excused himself to use the restroom. He got up and left.

A few seconds later another man came through her stream and was tangled, mangled in her hair.

The second guy bought her another drink.

The first guy came back, and for some reason, he looked at the second guy with such a face, one so horrid a tiger would run off and curl.

ROBERT M. DRAKE

The other guy took offense
and the next thing you know
these two men were rolling around on the ground, and
they almost killed each other over her attention.

That night I learned something far more valuable than
gold and diamonds.

How some women can start bigger fires than that of what
any forest known to man has remembered.

And since then, I am still burning.
I could barely remember how I got caught in her flame.

Sometimes things happen--without *you* knowing what has
just happened.

Some women can do that to a man.

WHAT THEY SEE

You can change someone's life.
Help them in ways they could have
never imagined.
Be there for them, save them
from the burning earth
and help them search for
what it is they love.

But they will only remember
that one moment you were not
there for them, and for whatever reason
it was.

Maybe you were running late,
you had too much on your own plate
or maybe you were out saving someone else.

They will only remember that *one* time
and break you into a million pieces
for that *one* time.

People are like that.
They pay close attention to the way you
fuck up more than anything else.

IT IS TOO HARD

"Oh, R. M. Drake, so many women follow you,
it must drive you mad, the way they talk about your
work and share it throughout the social media. It must
make all the men mad because it seems you can have all
their women and with very *little* effort."

"Very *little* effort?"

"This writing thing that lives inside me is as hard to
pour out as it is to even recognize. Besides, not only
women read my work but the men do too. What do people
take me as? A womanizer? That is no good. I write.
People either like it or they don't. It is all the same
to me."

"Yes, but the majority of your readers wear high
heels."

"What makes you think some men don't wear high heels?
It's a strange world filled with strange people." I
said. "And it doesn't take a genius to realize that."

GETTING YOUNGER

When I was young, I had so many things wrong
but that is the cost of youth:
you just don't get things as you should.

All our youth, we had been told what to do
and most of us hated that.
Our mayors and school teachers and priest would say:

"Do not do drugs. Do not drink alcohol--it can ruin
your life."

Don't do this or don't do that.

And of course, we did.
We did not want to end up like them.
Most of them looked miserable with worn-out eyes
as if they had seen too much or seen too little.

Too much of too little of anything can ruin you.

Too much love.
Too much company.
Too much work.
Too much studying.
Too much sex.
Too much thinking.

ROBERT M. DRAKE

It is no wonder why some of us
had no choice but to go to the drugs
or the alcohol. It made us feel
more human,
it made us, too much, for our own good.

FOR AMY

Listening to Amy Winehouse
on this Saturday afternoon.
The windows are open,
the doors are open,
and the fresh wind from the
west enters my living room.

There is not much to live
for, but if there is the slightest
possibility of having a
near perfect day, then maybe
it is today--on days like these.

When days like these pass--hell freezes over
and death stops to take note.

And all else,
well,
all else falls into place
a few seconds late,

as the music
and the wind carry on.

On days like these
I become more than

ROBERT M. DRAKE

just another story waiting
to run out of words.

I am becoming something the world
will remember: a book within a book
with a story to remarkable to put into words.

DO NOT BECOME THE WRITER

Do not become the writer.
Do not become that.
It is not easy to write.
Become a reader.
Learn from the writer.
Learn from the word.
It is much easier to live
as anything else,
but for the sake of your
own life,
do not become the writer.
All true writers live hard
and die even harder.

All true writers suffer a little
more than the average.

They see it all,
try to understand it all,
and sit there
in small rooms and write.

What a terrible passion
it is,

to live and write
and write and live,
so much that you barely
notice how to enjoy
the two.

Do not become the writer.

Most writers take their own lives.

They become mad.
They become the hunted.
They become all the things
they fight against.

Become anything else;
believe me,
any other art gets off the
hook too easily.

Writing is for those
who do not understand
anything else,
but the words and the pages
that come together
to remind the rest of the
world why
they exist in the first place,

why we are all
still here.

BEAUTIFUL AND DAMNED

But please,
do not become the writer
There are so many other things
you *can* do.

YOU GOT THIS

"I don't think I can go on."

"Kid, you have got to
pick yourself up
and stop all of this crying.
Sooner or later
you are going to forget
what it was that began
all of this hurting--all of this
unwanted sadness."

"But what if it never leaves?"

"All things leave, just like
all things change. Now
pick yourself up and begin.
Once you have learned
how to walk over
your insecurities,
your pain will not matter,
nothing will hurt you."

"Now carry on, your heart
can still be a beautiful place."

BOOK STORES

Walking in and out of
libraries and book stores

and suddenly, I am saddened
by the brutal reality,
that most, if not all, writers
in here have all suffered
a bit more.

All writers love hard.
All writers go on to live
and die alone.

And when their time here is done,

all they have left are their words.
Their words printed on pages
that will go on,
and go on through the ages.

And sadly, most will go on to be ignored.
Most will go on to be forgotten,

like the dreams we wake
to never remember again.

I AM HOLDING YOU INSIDE

Sitting here,
next to you,
I have come
to the conclusion
how it is all the same.
From stars to people,
we are all
drowning
in a pool
filled with too much
to handle.

Too much stress,
too much fear, and
it rises like the vapor
that escapes from our
lungs and burst into
nothing, into air.

It is all the same,
and it all ends the same.

From stars to people,
we die within ourselves,
waiting for whatever it is
our souls are made of

BEAUTIFUL AND DAMNED

to claim us and soften
us up to drift away
into the sky.

Sitting here,
next to you,
I have come to the
conclusion,
how it is all the same.
From the stars to the people,
we are all
struggling with parts
of ourselves
we are too afraid
to reveal.

TOO MUCH BROTHER

"But my brother drank with death
and the essence of life appeared closer."

"What do you mean?"

"What I am trying to say is,
he did not care about anything.
He was already dead,
or so it seemed, to the point where
nothing shook him."

"He must have been crazy."

"Yea, maybe he was
or maybe he wasn't,
but that does not matter.
He died a few months ago
and for some odd reason
I can feel him closer,
more than before."

"Maybe he is not dead."

"Yeah, maybe he is not, who knows."

THE DEATHLY YEARS

The years can really slow you down.

Sometimes it takes
something terrible
to get you going.
Something ugly,
something only the mad can
appreciate.

The years can really slow you down.

We sit here, my comrades,
and I after all these years
sitting in the porch
in front of Joe's house.

We laugh because
nothing has changed.
We laugh because we are
the beautiful and the damned.

The years can really slow you down.

And like all old men,
we sit there
and dream of all the

women we
wish we could have
had.

ON DAYS LIKE THESE

The days have become
far more dangerous than before.
The chaos,
the madness,
all of these things
piling on the corners
of the earth.
The people move toward
whatever it is that is safe.
No where is safe.
Safety is a state of mind
that only the blind find
peace in its comfort.

The noise is all around,
the guns and the bombs
and the silent terror
of the hurting children.
No one ever seems to care,
not unless it happens
to them,
and then, it automatically becomes
important, a problem.

But other than that,

we watch as it all
goes to hell.
We watch as it all
erases itself.

We watch
and yet, we remain perfectly still,
frozen inside
the hidden parts
of ourselves.

As man crumbles
and the legend it birthed
becomes...

Another lost echo
expanding in the
thrust of the mind.

SOCIAL MEDIA

My work is spreading
all over social media
and it is one of those things
that cannot be stopped--like falling in love
or falling out of love.

The reason why it is so popular?
Who knows
but I am sure love
has something to do with it.

The love I have for the art
and the people who love the art
and the art that speaks to the people
and the people
that speak to me.

Well, that is love,
that is special,
and that is something too
hard to stop.

You cannot un-remember someone.
You cannot un-touch someone,
un-fuck someone, un-know someone.

That is not how it works,
but this is how it works.

Work hard.
Fight hard.
Love hard.

And let the goodness
bloom out of your heart
like the forgotten flowers
that do not grow here.

Do all that you love, with
love and then...

drink to these things.
Live for these things.
Die for these things,
because of *these* things.

There will be no other
lecture after that.

Love is the root of all things
that are shared.

My work and yours.

KARMA IS A BASTARD

I had a guy buy five books of mine.
I remember him because he was so antsy about the books
and having them signed for his girlfriend.

"Do not forget to sign the books."

Broken records would have stopped to hear this guy,
this I tell you.

I made an effort to get them out as soon as possible,
the faster the better, I know people like him could
start a fire or draw a crowd or do something far more
terrible, like start a war.

I mailed them out and two weeks passed, of course, I
thought that was the end of it.

The following week I got an email from the same guy.

"I am missing two of the five books I ordered. What do
you plan to do about this?"

I should have let the world fall over his head.

"I will give you a refund for the two books."

Of course, it would have been impossible to remember if
I actually mailed those out correctly. I mail out
hundreds of books per week, but I could have sworn to
the breath in me that I *did*--do his order correctly.

I send over the refund and that was the end of it,
although I felt like I was not wrong here.

I kept an eye on him...

A week later he posts, through the social media, a
picture of all five books, *that bastard tricked me.*

It is okay though, the universe has a way of making
wrongs, right, and it never misses; believe me, once
you set it off-track it is bound to align itself on its
own.

Two weeks after that, someone had broken into his car
and stole his book bag with his work laptop and all of
my books.

It is all so lovely, and the way
things pan out is far more *deserving.*

I guess karma has a funny way of
coming through the door,
especially sooner than we expect it to come.

I hope whoever took those books *enjoyed them.*

THE GIRL IN THE ROOM

"That girl is crazy,
all she does is sit there and do nothing,"
one kid whispered to another.

I sat there listening in; I did that most of the time.

"That ~~girl will~~ eat your heart
and your brain, she's crazy. Just stay away from her."

She had a defeating awkwardness to her.
She ate in the lunch room alone and
she always wore black.

Black lipstick.
Black fingernails.
Black hair.
Black all around.

"She's a fucking witch."

Darn kids now-a-days are so quick to judge. They
will do anything for a little acceptance.

Acceptance is not the answer, at least *not* most of the
time.

ROBERT M. DRAKE

If you belong to a crowd, you are not free.

Freedom is the essence. Not many get this, although
they think they do but they do not.

Another boy passed by and sits next to the girl wearing
all black.
He sits beside her and smiles.

"Look at them, they are both freaks.
Stay the hell away from them!"

Maybe I am sitting in the wrong table. It seems like I
am.

Sometimes the loudest is the one who is not saying
anything at all.

THE THINGS WE FEEL

"I feel empty sometimes."

"We all do at times and that
happens when something
within us is shifting."

"Shifting?"

"Yes, with all that space inside us,
we are bound to be stirred up
from time to time."

"I don't understand."

"No one does kid,
just know that you do not have to
look towards the stars
to find incredible things.
Understand that there are things
inside you, colliding every second,
and they are offering you
about a thousand different
second chances
every single day."

ANYTHING GOES

Anything could happen here.

Maybe you will find someone
and fall in love.
But of course,
just like everyone else,
you keep spending most of your time
looking.

And you have been looking
hard enough, so hard
that when it finally arrives,
you barely remember what it was
you were looking for.

And

when it comes to you (because it will)
it will usually arrive beyond the expectation,
and you,
like the person you never knew,

ignore it.

It comes close enough,
and it is all, too fast to hold.

BEAUTIFUL AND DAMNED

and then, you,
like the person you never knew-you do nothing,
you say nothing,
and think nothing...

as you watch the love of your life
pass you by.

LITTLE WINDOWS

The time has gone
out the window,
and the inspiration
flows where the smoke blows,
in almost all directions.

These days, all continuing,
ultimately feel the same.
They have gone far out of place
and now
most of the time, what is inside us,
feels like empty roads
and torn maps that lead
to nowhere.

And it is a riot
because now I feel free to feel
almost anything.

To feel like time
has slipped through the cracks
of these walls.
It is gone, but it has also arrived
in a different light,
in a different train with different shades.

BEAUTIFUL AND DAMNED

But that is nothing new.
In order to let yourself go
within yourself,
you must reinvent yourself
and rise above the old
places you have created inside.

Rise,
the machine in *you* needs
more room to run.

Sometimes you have to self-destruct
in order to self-discover
and understand that
the only person
you must learn to let go
is *you*.

ANOTHER TRUE STORY

True story.

This woman I met,
she wants to run away.
She says she has had enough.
She has been putting up
with the bullshit people bring.

She does the wrong thing;
they burn her alive.
She does the right thing;
they burn her alive.

There is no end to their circus.

I tell her not to worry about
people, you cannot control
them, people will be people.

But something could always
be done and not many know this secret,
but I gave it to her anyway.

I leaned over and whispered
in her ear.

BEAUTIFUL AND DAMNED

"This is how you deal with them."

Control yourself.
Love yourself.
Pay attention to yourself.
While everyone else is
focusing on you,
you focus on you.
While they try to destroy,
you create, then create some more.
And they will remember you.
People like that will always
remember you.

Show them you are more.
The goal is not to defeat them.
The goal is to make them
understand.

THE GENTLE MADNESS

The night is where people like us belong.

The night will always call our names.

Not many will understand this;
many will think we are crazy.

We used to stay up late for no reason and we were up
till the sun would wake; this I remember.

There were times when we were apart, but I knew you
were up, perhaps, even doing the same thing I was
doing.

I can still remember those late nights. The times we
would lay in bed and count the ridges on my ceiling.
They were like small mountains mounted above our heads.
Those late nights were really something, this I tell
you. I miss them and now they flash through my memory
like fireworks blooming in the middle of the sky and it
hurts.

It always hurts.

The slow sting of watching you come and go, those
moments probably hurt the most--like spending a few

hours with you was *never* enough. We always wanted more
and even if we had more, it still, was never enough.

And it will never be.
And I cannot make sense of this crave.
This urgent want,
this heavy little feeling of *missing you.*

I miss you.

I feel like the night still belongs to us;
and it calls my name.
It keeps haunting me.
It gets under my skin, breaking the atoms of what once
was,
and what will never be.

I still remember you.

You are in my head when no one else is around.
You are the ticking of a clock: the seconds remind me
of you.

The night is where people like *us* belong.
It is the only place where we could feel free.

The only place where we do not need light,
and still, we could both see where we should be.

I miss you

and sometimes, I wonder if *you* miss me.

And that is the only thing
I really want to know.

If I am in your mind in the middle of the night,
where it is, where I belong.

LIGHT AND BLACK HOLES

To the one I let slip away.

You bought out
the things that made me real.

All the failures,
the ugly and the wrongs.

No one ever wants to talk
about the wrongs.
Most ignore it,
until it happens to them,
then suddenly it becomes
truth, it becomes life.

Why do good things have to end?
And why do most good things have to
end bad?

When we were good, for a moment,
I would have thought world
peace broke out.

There was no war,
no bloodshed across the globe
nor in my own home.

ROBERT M. DRAKE

To the one I let slip away.

It was me that let you go.
If it were any other way,
then perhaps, you would have
fed me to the wolves.

All good things must end,
they must, there is no way around it.

And now, like all who have
seen too much, I sit here
in solitude wondering about
the past.

The body finds peace.
The mind finds peace.
Now the heart, now *that* is
where war is continuous,
that is where you will hear screams
no one has ever heard.

And

we could have kissed
the gods, my dear.
We could have been two suns
lighting up the sky
but moving on is a bitch,
and now, it is too late.

GLASS DOESN'T BREAK

I need to forget you,
the same way you need to
forget me but the songs
I keep playing do not stop
bringing us back from the grave
and the photographs do not stop
giving me life.

Goddamn, look at me now,
I am not even sure what I have become?

I go out for a drink with my comrades and all I can do
is think about you, think about us,
and how I keep fucking up.

Hell, this is almost everything I write about now. I
have become dim
and the inspiration has lost its way; it has nowhere to
go.

I pour more drinks.
I am one drink from being an alcoholic. My comrades
scream in cheer.

I need to forget you.
I need to forget.

ROBERT M. DRAKE

Forget you.
Any more of you in my brain
is deadly.

The drinks stay in me.
You stay in me.

I am dying:
in my brain and in my heart.

I have died a thousand times
and not a soul to notice

the happenings that are
happening within.

PEOPLE LIVE IN CAMERAS

People are not pictures;
they are not the music they create
or the art they create.
They are not the things you see
in the museum halls,
the things the academia worship
and print on books.

No, *none* of that.

People are the flashes,
the split second before the picture is taken.
The instruments they use to conduct such sounds.
The paint they use to capture the colors.

People are more than that
of what they leave behind.
More than that of what they create.

They are museums themselves
and most, if not all, have more
to offer then they think.

Pay close attention; appreciate
every movement, every thought
and every reaction from the people around you.

ROBERT M. DRAKE

Do it daily.

Remember. Remember. Remember.

You never know,
today might be their last.

BELIEVE IN MAGIC

The first time soul mates meet,
there is magic.
When someone saves a life,
there is magic.
When a mother gives birth,
there is magic.
When you find God,
there is magic.

Believe me. It is there.

When all hope was lost,
I found magic.

I wrote 800 pages of prose
in a 500 square foot apartment
in three years.

800 pages to move millions of people.

Now *that is magic.*

With no hot water,
no cable television
and barely any food.

ROBERT M. DRAKE

With almost nothing
to hang on to--just a dream.

I found magic.

My words, whatever it is they are.
I know they come from a lineage
of magic.

Now some do not believe this
but there is magic everywhere,
even here, in a small room with
little to no hope in.

All you have to do is believe
and keep those eyes peeled
and wait.

Always wait.

Something magical is bound
to happen.

Believe me.

THE THINGS WE DON'T SAY

"It hurts so much."

"What does?"

"Watching the horrors of the world,
the videos on social media,
the people dying--the screams."

"Don't watch them."

"I can't ignore it; they are everywhere I go.
I wish I can do something about the pain."

"There is always something you can do. Believe me."

And that is the great dilemma.
The problem we all face today
with the terror.

No one knows what to do.
No one knows how they can help

but

there is a way to defeat it
and that is by not ignoring it.

ROBERT M. DRAKE

By talking about it
and spreading it like free
laughter in a dull day.

Every time you shed a light
on it, the distance towards peace
becomes a little more visible.

So share it.
Talk about it.
The more we see it,
the easier it will be
to recognize it before it gets
out of control.

1999

Damn police always abusing their power
but there are some things that are far worse.

When I was younger, we used to write our names on the
walls like champions.

One night, like every other night,
my comrades and I went through the Bleau for a little
late night session.

We had spray cans of all colors.

The night went well and we were just about done.

On the car ride back, one of my comrades decided to
"get up" one more time. He got off the truck while the
rest of us waited in the truck parked by a
neighborhood.

It was dark and no one was around.

He walked on the side walk by 8th street and 107th
avenue, right by Florida international University.

A copped flew by; he must have been going at least 100
miles an hour.

Cops can do that. Go over the speed limit in a school
zone, no one does anything to cops; they sometimes make
their *own* laws.

My comrade goes and makes sure the cop clears the
street.

He began to spray the wall. The cop turned on his
sirens and makes a u-turn.

"Fuck dip... dip... dip..."

He ran back toward us as my other comrade puts the
truck in reverse.

You would have thought this was a scene from a movie.

The red and blue flashes consumed the scene.
The cops slammed his breaks right in front of us, while
my other comrade ran off with the spray can on his
hand.

The cop pulls a gun on us,
took us out of the car and slammed us onto the
pavement.

He was cursing and cursing.

"You little shit-fucks like writing on other people's
property?"

BEAUTIFUL AND DAMNED

He grabbed the can and sprayed my comrade's truck.

About 3 whole minutes passed
and two other cop cars pulled in.

Now like I said, you would have thought there was a
camera rolling because four more cops pulled in and
they beat us numb.

They even sent one of us to the hospital.

Now it was either a beating or go to juvenile hall and
let our parents eat us alive, and believe me; anything
was better than that.

The wrath our parents would have brought would have
made that police beating look like a beautiful summer
day.

DO IT FOR YOURSELF

Play your music loud.
Drive your car fast.
Talk about your movies all day.
Drink your coffee in public.
Draw your paintings
in the middle of a lecture.

You do all these things,
and they make you feel something.

Well, that is *alright*.

Just make sure you are doing
all these things for you
and not for them. (The people around you.)

Do things because they
speak to you,
and you speak to them.
Not for *them* to know what you are doing.

For you. For you. For you.

It is all, after all, all about you,
and please for the love of life,
do not be like most.

BEAUTIFUL AND DAMNED

Most live for other people.
Most starve for attention,
because to them, attention is more valuable than life.

Believe me, for this,
people would kill one another

but you--you have got to
do it for yourself,
and you will bring yourself back
from the madness.

The crowd will *never* get this.
They will never understand
why you are *everything*.

THE STRANGE THINGS IN STRANGERS

Goddamn it, sometimes life is beyond beautiful--beyond
anything you can imagine, but even so,
you always expect more.

Then perfection happens and time happens, and that
perfection becomes dull and old. And then, another
perfect moment sweeps you of your feet.

I was in a crowded bar in Wynwood, full of nine-to-
fivers, hipsters and people looking for cheap love.

I looked across the room.
It was one of those reactions,
you know, when you look towards your side because it
feels like someone is looking at you
without knowing if someone
is even there.

I sharply turned over
and there, I saw a woman staring right back at me.

She smiled and then I smiled.
She came over to my side of the room

and I noticed her lips were filled with the color of
broken love.

I knew that color; there was no mistake in it. I, too,
had been wearing it for nearly a year: on and off.

She walks as if she had been walking all her life, and
walking towards something that has, too, been walking
all its life. (She will never catch *it*!)

"I know who you are..."

She smiled again and took the moon from me.

We talked for a moment,
but one thing really caught
my attention.

"I feel everything you write.
You are not alone."

For some time now, I had been writing to make myself
feel better about myself and what I had been feeling
lately.

No one ever wants to feel alone.

I write for the *goddamn* connection.

That night, I realized I was there for the same reason she was there--to ease the reality we both were trying to escape from.

"Your writing has saved me from suicide." She mentions over and over.

In that moment, I realized she had saved me, at least for that one night.

BE ANYONE, EVEN YOU

A random girl in a hospital
came to talk to me.

"I hit my head and now
I cannot remember who I am."

"That is what makes you beautiful." I said.

I smiled and nodded my head.

"How so?" she asked.

Her eyes were filled with so much reality;
I almost lost sense of my very own.

"Because right now...
you can be anyone, even *you*."

I, TOO, GO MAD

I have gone through
at least ten typewriters
this past year,
two laptops and several
other things I use on a daily basis.

Now it is not in me to break things I use.
It is just when they do not work
I tend to lose my cool.

I break words.
I break thoughts.
I break anything that does
not want to cooperate.

I am filled with rage and it
only takes a moment to set
it off in all the wrong places.

My hands become destructive things--
wild things, violent things--
like a pack of wolves piercing through
the pits of hell.

So when you tell me
I can learn how to love you,

BEAUTIFUL AND DAMNED

that you see the goodness in me,
it only means you see what
you want to see.

But most are like that,
I cannot blame you.

I just need you to understand
how your heart
is not in safe hands.
If I must, I will break it,
and if I must,
I will even break my own.

THE TRUTH IS SOMETHING ELSE

One Sunday afternoon I am here talking to my nephew. He
rants about new shoes, new shirts and new video games.

"Listen, love--
that's what they want you to do.
They want you to obsess
on their untruthfulness.
The brands they sell you are not true.
They want you to look, act, and feel a certain way. A
way that makes *them* feel safe."

"They want you to work all week long, stress and then
go out on the weekend; buy their brands to make
yourself feel good about yourself."

"Wow, I never thought about it that way."

"Of course, you wouldn't, that's not how it works. If
they told you the truth, the ugly truth, then perhaps,
you wouldn't support their brands. They want you for
your all, as long as they are profiting, they could
care less if what they sell you kills you. And that
right there is the truth."

I CANT GIVE YOU THIS

No one ever really wants to save someone else. That's
too much work. You can start off with an infinite
amount of enthusiasm, but it all ends in exhaustion.

You cannot save other people.
You cannot destroy other people.

And no one can do these things to you as well.

You want to save the world?

Try saving yourself--day by day,
night in, day out.

Every day, the mirror
screams, "save me."
And you do not have to say it back;
your eyes tell it to yourself.

Save yourself;
only you have the power to do so.

Only you have the power to destroy
or build, or re-build.

That God-like power is in you.

THE WOLVES IN YOU

Give yourself a little credit.
Do you know how hard it is to wake up in the morning:
get dressed, eat something and go to work for almost 10
hours?

Give yourself a little credit.
Do you know how hard it is *not* to kill someone in the
middle of traffic,
or in the middle of the crowd?

Give yourself a little credit.
Do you know how hard it is to pay high rent, high gas,
and high living expenses?

Give yourself a little credit.
Do you know how hard it is to live?
How hard it is to like people, the things you have to
do to get by?

Give yourself a little credit.
Give yourself a moment,
to realize how strong you really are before going back
to the chaos of the world.

Sometimes a moment
is all we have

BEAUTIFUL AND DAMNED

and sometimes it is what we need
to toughen us up
before sending us back to the wolves.

THE WAIT FOR SOMETHING TO HAPPEN

A boy and his grandfather
were out sitting in the bus stop.
The boy asks.

"Why are you so quiet today, eh?"

The grandfather disoriented, slowly responds.

"There is such a sound
coming from the silence
and if you listen closely
it will hit you like a
speeding train
and leave you right where
it found you."

"Can you hear that?
Something is coming and
it is angry."

"What is it?" the boy asked.

There was a group of young women jogging down the side
walk and heading our way.

BEAUTIFUL AND DAMNED

All three of us sat in silence as
if words did not exist.

They passed through us,
and we sat there,
and our heads turned like gears.

That day I understood how
there are some things, no matter how old you are, you
just understand.

That's life and sometimes that's love,

but you don't need *this* to understand
that.

ROBERT M. DRAKE

CLOCKS THAT DON'T TICK

If there is something to be done
before your clock meets its end,
then it is this:

*Take in everything with such appreciation and deep
adoration. It is all such a gift,
all of it, all of this.*

Even the goddamn way you drink,
sleep, talk, laugh, work,
drive to work is something we all should appreciate.

Every second within the seconds
should be well spent.

There is a time for everything,
and that is very true.

But *everything* should be appreciated.

Let that feeling of fullness
knock on your head
and starve your heart from the bullshit lies.

Appreciate that,
and this and everything in-between.

BEAUTIFUL AND DAMNED

It will give you thunder
when it rains
and it will be the only thing
that separates you from the dead.

ROBERT M. DRAKE

THE MURDER OF TREES

My name is on the paper again
and the more is appears, that harder it is for me to
live.

I get sprouts of emails and phone calls: they come in
waves.

Back and forth they go on to praise what I am doing, to
tell me how *magnificent* I am.

I do not see that
and the paper sees what they want to see.

The truth is, I am no one.
I barely have a dream to hang on to; the paper and the
media make it hard for me to go on. And the praise the
people give me sometimes feels like a rude awakening.

I do not know why it is like this,
and I do not want to know either.

It is just hard for me to take all in
but of course, I do not expect anyone to understand
this.

BEAUTIFUL AND DAMNED

If it is not written on the paper or streamed on the television, then no one will *believe* it.

Most people only *believe* what they are feed, even if it comes in that form.

In the end, no one will see my sorrow; people will believe what they want to believe...

My name printed on sheets of paper, meant to define me for all that makes me and all that I am.

DELY WELY

My 13-year-old niece--
she *gets it*.

She sees me stressed out,
sitting downstairs behind
my desk (the one where
I do most of my writing.)

She walks up to me
and asks.

"How have you been?
You don't look so well."

"It's just been a tough week."

Her small face tilts
and with bright eyes like
a street lamp--she smiles.

She says,

"It's always a tough week.
It's just sometimes
you don't realize it.
You have to learn

BEAUTIFUL AND DAMNED

how to separate the bad
from the worse
and find those little moments
of happiness in-between,
and if you can have
enough of those each day,
then that would be enough
to get you through the week."

She nods her head
and walks away.

I smile, lost in a faraway stare
and I am reminded of how beautifully tragic
life is.

Sometimes, a moment
can take you away
and sometimes, it takes you
far enough--to where the sky is dark
and there is no light,
but the birds still spread their wings
and fly.

And all we do is point them out
as we watch them caress the sky.

SILENT BOMBS

The baby is crying,
louder than ever, with a note so hard and deep you
would swear the dead would rise to ask me to shut her
off.

The baby is crying,
and her face, filled with the color red,
with so much rage and expansion...
you would think there are at least 100 super nova's in
her, exploding and bursting for a way out.

The baby is crying,
she moves her tiny limbs with such force and
electricity--I sometimes think her energy can fill at
least four city blocks, and I wonder how much fire is
trapped inside of her small body.

The baby is crying,
her eyes do not open. She keeps them closed as she
breaks the cord and riots like she is busting out of
jail.

The baby is crying.
The sky is crying.
The people are crying.
Your eyes are crying.

BEAUTIFUL AND DAMNED

And still,
the baby is crying,
and it is all alright
because I, too, am crying.
We all are crying,
but the difference is
some of us go unheard.

TWO STONES, ONE LAKE

Two older men are sitting on a bench in a mall as their
wife's shop in the same department store.

They both eavesdrop on this young couple arguing over
what movie to see.

The couple walks off into the madness of the crowd.

The two men smirk at each other as if they understood a
something the rest of the world didn't get.

One of them leans over with his golf hat and musty
beard.

"That's it, that's how it goes, that's true love. Have
you ever been in love?" he asks.

The other man puts his new paper down.

"No, not really, because every time I believe to be, it
ends badly." he replies.

"But isn't that the way it's meant to go? Isn't that
the way all musicians, poets and painters have
interpreted it?"

"I believe so, but maybe they're wrong. Maybe we're all wrong and we don't have the slightest clue on what it's really about. The lie of love is one to believe the moment you want to believe in the lie, but I can see through all of that."

"Yeah, I suppose you might have stuck gold there."

"Yeah, I believe that, too."

"So, what do you *really* think about your wife?"

"I think she's insane, and you?

"I think mine is insane, as well."

The man with the news paper gets up, tucks his shirt and gives a goodbye to the other man. His wife was waiting for him by the exit.

"Good luck." said the man still waiting.

"Same to you."

They both went their separate ways and never did the men think about what they had just talked about. They just held it in and went on with their lives.

TAKE EVERYTHING

This woman I never met, I just admired for a few
moments while being at the gas station.

Tall like some warrior goddess sent to slay men. Her
hair, fiery, mixed with reds and browns: a light tone
of each.

Her face looked serious while she was pumping her gas.
Strong and stone-like, like a statue waiting for the
earth to fall on her shoulders.

She is beautiful without a doubt,
but she seemed like she was so deep into her own world,
that perhaps, she was either on top of it or the only
one left to survive it.

She took a look at me, of course she would, I was
literally in front of her, but she couldn't see what I
was seeing. I was wearing Ray-Bans and it was as bright
as a popped neon glow stick in the dark.

She stopped pumping her gas, jumped in her car and
drove off.

How sad that I will never see her again.
So many stories to know that I will never understand,

it is like she doesn't exist, but maybe she does or maybe she doesn't. I wouldn't be the one to call that.

I still remember that day--that encounter was over 17 years ago--in 1999 when I got my first car. It's funny how you can remember a complete stranger but you hardly think about the people you see every day.

Every day is taken for granted and every day we are closer to death and only in death do we wish we had at least one last day left.

ROBERT M. DRAKE

GIRLFRIENDS AND GIRLS

When we were kids, all we would talk about was having a girlfriend and when my cousin finally had one, it left him distorted for a while.

"So how did it feel?"

"It filled me whole and then it left me quicker than the sky flying the clouds."

"It was that bad?"

"Yeah, but that's what it's all about. The urgency of another person, someone you know--you will never live to see again. It hurts, it's like a pain hidden within other chambers of pain and somehow I'm attracted to it all."

"Hell, that doesn't sound too good at all. It sounds like a tragedy."

"Yeah, love will do that to you."

"Do what?" I said.

"It will nearly kill you and leave you barely alive, *enough* for you to come back for more."

357

Over the years, he had nearly died several times and every time he came back he was a different person. A few years later, I finally understood the fire and it nearly killed me too, and I haven't been the same person since. I guess, in a lot of ways he was *right*.

ROBERT M. DRAKE

SUNDAY IS NOT A FUN DAY

My friend, on a cold Sunday afternoon randomly reads one of my prose's about death. It was about how I do not care of it, "if it happens then it happens."

"Are you afraid of death?" she asked as if it was the last question on earth.

"No, because the dead don't know they're dead. The memory is in the brain. If the brain is off, then it is all off." I replied.

"So, you don't believe in the afterlife?" she grabbed her tea mug and took two sips before putting it back down on the table.

"Probably not, my brother died in 2014 and ever since I do not care much of it."

"Wow, that's recent, my condolences."

"Sometimes, when I think about death, it feels as if death is right around the corner, waiting to sneak up on me. I mean that's how death works. No one ever knows when it's going to happen and when it does--it comes gently and silently like a long whisper flying through our ears."

BEAUTIFUL AND DAMNED

We didn't say a word for a few minutes and quickly
changed the subject as we continued to drink our tea.

Death will do that to you.
Take the life out of your mouth
and leave you with nothing
but a cold brew on a cold Sunday afternoon.

FOR ANDI

How many times have I brought myself back from the dead?

It must be at least 16 times so far,
resurrected 16 times to see the moon as new 16 times
and so on.

It is the art that is my savior
and I am not alone.

The other night in the Wynwood Walls, a young girl
recognized me from the crowd and approached me.

She slowly spoke with a gloom in her words.

"Your poetry has got me through some really rough
times. It has saved my life." (I get that a lot.)

I looked at her with eyes as raw as the hidden truth,
with a heart that has died a few times and smiled at
her.

"It has saved me a couple of times too." I replied.

It is moments like these that make coming back to the
world something easy to do.

LOVE ONLINE

An ex-lover would always get on my case with social media. She would always go off and rant.

"Why can't you put you're in a relationship with me online?"

Goddamn, it drove me mad. At times, I wanted to erase the whole social media thing because of it. Every week it was always the same thing. Over and over. The moon would have turned its face to avoid her complaining.

"Hell, you are here with me aren't you?
We see each other daily don't we?
What is the deal with you and putting that online? What gives?"

"It makes me feel secure about our relationship."

"Makes you feel secure?" that kind of security blew my mind.

"Yes, it does."

Some people, I swear, are so insecure about themselves they need some kind of validation. It is almost the same with people you know or think you know.

"But you don't follow me on social media."

All of that drives me mad. "We are friends in real life
aren't we?"

Some people, I swear, are so insecure with their
goddamn boring lives that they need anything to make
them feel more in control.
Anyway, the following day I got rid of her and the
social media as well.

Now all else makes sense, at least for now.

ONE DAY LIKE ALL DAYS

On January 17th, 2015...

I came home drunk,
barely alive from a wild Friday night
and I stared at the mirror
and I knew you were on the other side.
I almost felt as if you were going through the same
thing as me.

I knew you were thinking of me,
thinking, if I was thinking of you
in that very moment of the night as well.
And I *was thinking of you*
and in a strange way, that made
me feel as if we were still connected.
Maybe it is all in my head
or maybe it is not.

The universe has a funny way
of telling you things and that alone made me
feel as if I was not alone.

You were right there with me.

You are the ghost to all those
lonely nights that haunt me.

364

You are *everything* that the living
has never done before.

GODSEND

Two women sit in a bar.

One goes off on the other about her older sister.
She rambles and rambles.

"I can't believe my sister. She is always on her phone.
While we are having lunch, she is on her damn phone.
While we are in the mall, she is on her damn phone.
Hell, when she is in the restroom, she is on her
goddamn phone. I don't get it and it drives me crazy."

"Maybe she's looking for something?"

"What could she possibly be looking for online? You
can't find anything meaningful there."

"Well, that's a ridiculous way to see things, because
the times are changing. Now you can find anything
online, even love."

MARIA DIED AND I WASN'T SORRY

"Did you recognize Maria today?"

"Sort of, she seemed a bit different but barely."

"She is different. Before, figuratively speaking, the
clouds would wrap around her hair and a few moons would
circulate her head--in sequence too. But today, today
she looks like she has carried herself to the end of
herself. And I could tell by the way she came in
today."

"You can?"

"Yes, it is indefinitely."

"So what happen to her?"

"No one knows. She's just someone else."

"Someone else?"

"Yeah, she must have had enough.
She must have killed the old her
and came back anew."

"How is that even possible?"

"That's easy, champ; almost everyone dies a few times in their lives. And those who do, never speak about it, it's just one of those things others who have died a few times pick-up on. *We understand each other.*"

"Whoa, I don't get that."

"Well, of course you don't, and you have got some *dying* to do."

FOR HEXDIESEL

Sitting here in my brother's eulogy,
his body like a fallen statue placed back into the
dirt, where we all come from.
I see everyone, frozen at the fact that he is gone.
Some have accepted it, while others still couldn't
believe it; even some till this day can't believe it.

My cousin Hex leans over and whispers quietly.

"I don't even know what to say or feel."

"I think a lot of us have nothing left to feel." I say.

"What do you mean? How does it feel when you have
nothing left to feel?"

"It feels like having the feelings pulled out of your
body without them even being ready to be let go."

He paused and raised his eye brow as he delicately swam
in a pool filled with confusion. *I don't expect anyone
to feel the same way about this.*

"It sort of feels a lot like right now, like knowing
someone you love no longer inhabits the earth and
standing before them as they go."

"I can imagine that." he said.

"You don't need to imagine it; you are living in that moment, right now."

LOVE YOU LIKE FOREVER

Kevin was Janet's best friend.
He had known her since grade school. He was always
there for her no matter what. They both had gone
through the fire and had gone back a few times around.

Little did Janet know how much Kevin felt for her, it
was so great-that Kevin himself barely knew it too, but
he always felt as if something was always there.

One night, drunk off white wine, they sat on the hood
of his car as they peered at the sky.

"Have you seen that movie..." she said.

"Which one?"

I can't remember, but Tom Hanks is in it and this other
lady..." She snaps her fingers as she tried to remember
the other actress' name.

"I don't know which one you're talking about." Kevin
laughed a little as he kept his eyes glues to the
mysteries of the night.

"It's magical. Every time they play it on TV it gives
me that, you know, at home feel."

"Yeah, but you don't need a movie to feel that, you know?"

"What do you mean?"

"There is always a small amount of magic running through the street and if you pay close attention you might see it."

"Really? How?"

"Well, I followed it and it brought me to you and now because of it, my quiet little world is filled with it."

"Filled with what?" she said, her eyes curious and her voice cracked a little as she asked her question.

"That same magic I'm talking
to you about. It explodes in the middle of the night
and sometimes,
when I'm lucky enough,
I could see it in the sky.
Like tonight--it's everywhere,
covering the spinning earth
all at once.
And I don't care if it vanishes
the next moment.
I'm here with you
and that's good enough for me.

ROBERT M. DRAKE

She leaned up against him
and looked at the sky.
And in that moment,
she felt at home.
And for the very first time,
she, too, saw that same magic,
and it illuminated the sky
like tiny riots of lights and from that night on, they
followed her everywhere she was meant to go.

THE PERFECT GIRL

I saw the *perfect girl*, one Wednesday afternoon.

She seemed to be interrupted today, interesting
nonetheless, but ultimately interrupted. Her face blue,
her arms and legs blue, even her eyes were filled with
the color of the sky.

"What's the matter? You are usually happy, what's with
the sudden attitude shift?" I asked.

She, being the majestically clever girl that she was
stayed quiet for a moment as she drank a cup filled
with soda. (We were sitting out back during our lunch
hour at work.)

"This life is meaningless," she said as she twirled her
straw in the cup.

The comment was odd, but relatively true. For some
reason, I, too, had my face blue, my arms and legs
blue, and even my eyes were the same damn color as the
sky.

"I feel what you are saying. Most times I feel as if I
don't know what I am doing, as if everything I do will
eventually lead me to nothing."

"Yes, my point exactly, this is why I say life is meaningless. Sometimes there isn't much meaning in the things we do, let alone the things we think."

"I agree but even feeling this way and saying life is meaningless is meaningless too. We are damned." I replied.

"Yes, we are beautiful and we are damned."

There was no further conversation after that. The next day she quit her job and no one ever heard from her. I guess our friendship was, in fact, meaningless because we *never* saw each other after that.

But she was *still* the perfect girl in my eyes.

SHE HAS ALL OF MY BOOKS

My friend, one who reads my words, one I send my words to on a daily basis, she, herself, finally dropped the bomb on me, but I expected that sooner or later.

She says,

"You shouldn't spend too much of your time writing."

"What do you mean? This is all I have."

"I mean, there is so much more out there, and all you do is stay in your small apartment and write and write and write, literally from sunrise to sunset. There is something off in you. You're missing life's point."

"But this is the only thing I understand. I don't understand anything else. I have to write as if it's my last day on earth, any moment I could die. I believe it is better to live your life doing what you love and dying by it too. Imagine that."

She paused for a few moments and she thought about it and there was nothing else to say about that.

NEW BOTTLES AND EMPTY ONES TOO

Drunk off the art
one night, frustrated
how the words could not
connect. I felt disconnected
and far away from
the flesh that makes me.

I think to myself
how I might not make
these deadlines to *write*
these *dead*-lines.

Quiet and alone,
chasing my very own shadow.
I think it is over.
My art and all I have created.

And then,
there she comes,
out of her own skin,
raw in love and away
from the ordinary.

BEAUTIFUL AND DAMNED

Even if for a moment,
I sometimes feel as if
I have lost the love for almost
all things.

But still, I love her
as she pieces herself
back together while she breaks
herself further apart.

And to be honest,
my days are numbered,
but watching her makes
me feel more
and there is nothing
more magnificent than that.

DREAMS CAN'T DIE

There are two inmates sharing laundry duties this week of December. Throughout the week they don't say a word to each other but today was not like any other day.

"How much time do you have left?" one of the men asked the other as he folds the clothes.

"I have about 33 days left. I've been in here for almost two years."

"Wow, not bad. What do you plan to do when you get out?"

"Nothing, find a job, a wife and probably have a child."

"That's sounds like a miraculous thing."

"What about you? How much do you have left? Young-blood."

"I'm in here for life, but if I keep up with the good behavior, maybe I'll see the sun again from the other side."

BEAUTIFUL AND DAMNED

And for those who want to end where they stand always
remember how there is hope *everywhere*.

Even in the belly of the beast.

NOTHING IS FOREVER

"They say when someone leaves, something inside of you
dies, but they also say something inside of you is
born."

That must had been the line that set me off, that set
off this whole writing gig.

My friend of 20 plus years called me over the
telephone.

Now I hate phone calls;
I hate text messages
and most of the time,
I hate communication period.
(Ironic enough?)

It had been a long time since we spoke. She was one of
those friends, the kind who disappear on you as soon as
they entered a relationship. I guess she had been going
through some tough waters because that's the only time
she would call me.

We did the casual talk and then we talked about what
she called me for, obviously.

BEAUTIFUL AND DAMNED

"I don't understand how you can spend so much time with
someone, and then, in an instant they are gone," she
said.

"That's life, people come and go." I said.

"I just don't feel the same anymore
and now I feel more trapped within myself... more than
ever, more than before." her voice trembled as if she
were living in fear.

"Because some people can do that to you, kid. Some
people can free you from yourself," I said.

Soon after we hung up and I replayed those two
sentences over and over...

*They say when someone leaves something inside of you
dies, but they also say something inside of you is
born.*

Like a windmill caught in a hurricane. Those words kept
cycling and cycling through my head, with no bound and
no end.

And I am still trapped within myself but I think
those were the wisest words I have ever heard.

AND NOW... AND NOW...

And now, they have departments
for everything you own.

For your car,
for your house,
for your kids,
for your money,
for your school
and even your own dreams.

And they can, if they wanted to,
take it all away. Not even the people you love belong
to you; death is always waiting in the back of the
show, that, and they want you to think it all belongs
to you.

And what a shame it is, how nothing is ever really
yours.

The only thing you own is your debt,
and you carry it with you as if it is pushed by your
skin.

Debt is inevitable...

BEAUTIFUL AND DAMNED

Nothing more.
Nothing less.

I DON'T HATE YOU

The last conversation is always the worse; this is something I have always believed.

But I ran into her a few years later and I discovered that the last conversation isn't the worse, it is the one you have--the next time you meet.

"Why did you help find me? If all you wanted to do was leave me behind?
Why did you love me? If in the end, you left all this pain behind?" She said.

I had nothing to say...

"I don't hate you. I don't hate anyone." She spoke again.

Shocked at the questions she was asking. She didn't even care to bother how I was doing. Women are like that at times, they don't forget, so please watch out with them.

"I just want to understand what it's like to be an *asshole* that is all." she said with the flames in her eyes more visible than before.

BEAUTIFUL AND DAMNED

I couldn't say a word. The words did not pour and that
was unusual--the words would always pour.

Sometimes, you are the *asshole* everyone warns you
about, even if you cannot *see* it for yourself.

To Charise:

May your flame live
within me,
and continue to
inspire me
through every
waking hour.

I can feel you flowing in me.

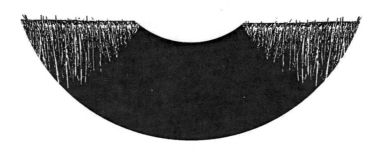

With open eyes I see the world,
with an open heart I see the souls
and with an open mind I see it all differently.

Thank you for your time.

Robert M. Drake

We will rebuild this world.

CHASING THE GLOOM

A NOVEL — FALL 2016

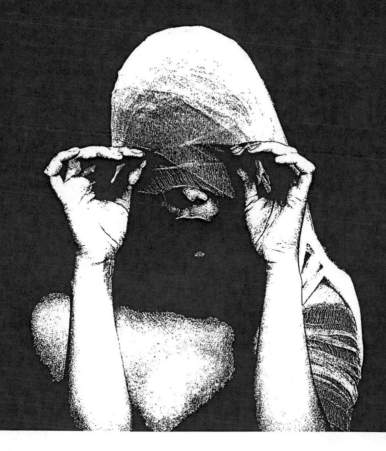

A BRILLIANT MADNESS

ROBERT M. DRAKE

BLACK BUTTERFLY

ROBERT M. DRAKE

beautifulCHAOS

ROBERT M.
DRAKE

SCIENCE

The Stars in Me are the Stars in You.

ROBERT M. DRAKE

ROBERT M. DRAKE

SPACESHIP

A Collection of Words for the Misunderstood.

Follow R. M. Drake
for excerpts and updates.

Facebook.com/RMDRK
Twitter.com/RMDRK
Instagram.com/RMDRK
RMDRK.Tumblr.com

For Gui,

One day I will find you
and we will laugh
and it will be as if
we are seeing each other
for the very first time.

Rest easy my brother.

CPSIA information can be obtained
at www.ICGtesting.com
Printed in the USA
LVOW12s0045240616

493738LV00002B/2/P